# Sarah Beth's Problem

## N. Geraldine Plunkett

Brethren Press

*Sarah Beth's Problem*
Copyright ©2003 N. Geraldine Plunkett
Published by Brethren Press, 1451 Dundee Avenue, Elgin, IL 60120.
Brethren Press is a program of the Church of the Brethren General Board.

Library of Congress Control Number: 2003111104
ISBN: 0-87178-055-0

07 06 05 04 03  5 4 3 2 1

Printed in the United States of America

# CONTENTS

CHAPTER 1

# The Problem

"Ouch!" Sarah Beth jerked her hand away from the cross hen's sharp beak. She set the basket of eggs down and gingerly lifted the big Dominicker off the nest.

No egg. Sarah Beth's frown turned into a smile. A cross hen sitting on a nest this late in the day without laying an egg meant one thing—a settin' hen—a hen that was ready and eager to hatch a brood of baby chicks.

Sarah Beth picked up the basket of eggs and hurried to the house. "Mama," she said, "there's a settin' hen in the chicken house. Last fall you promised I could have a settin' of eggs come spring. You said that if I cared for a brood of chickens and raised them by myself, all the money from the sale of the fryers would be mine. Can I have a settin' of eggs now?" Sarah Beth's words flew from her mouth as fast as grains of wheat spewing from a threshing machine at harvest time.

Mama smiled at her daughter's excitement. "Let's wait a day or two to be sure the hen stays on the nest," Mama suggested. "Then you may have your settin' of eggs."

"How many eggs can I have?" Sarah Beth wanted to know. "I think the old Dominicker is the biggest of all the hens. She can cover a lot of eggs. Do you think maybe thirty eggs?"

Mama laughed. "I doubt if any hen can keep that many eggs warm enough to hatch. We'll see if she can cover two dozen. Even that might be a stretch."

While drying the supper dishes, Sarah Beth told Grandma about the settin' hen and the promise of a settin' of eggs. "How much money do you think I'll get for twenty-four fryers?" Sarah Beth asked.

"Shush, child, don't get ahead of yourself," Grandma cautioned. "It's way too soon to answer that question."

That wasn't the kind of answer Sarah Beth wanted to hear. When the last pan was dried and put away, Sarah Beth and Grandma went into the living room.

Daddy had lit the kerosene lamp on the round table and was reading the newspaper. Lynwood was doing his homework, and Mama was reading nursery rhymes to Will.

Sarah Beth had finished her homework at school while Mrs. Davis was working with the fifth-grade class. Now she took the big Sears mail-order catalog from the bookcase and laid it on the table. It fell open to a page in the toy section—a page to which Sarah Beth had opened the thick book again and again.

Sarah Beth glanced at the dollhouse in the catalog. If she raised a brood of chickens, surely she would be able to buy that dollhouse. But it was no longer the house she wanted. It was just a puny little thing with only four rooms.

Sarah Beth unfolded a page that she had tucked into the Sears catalog—an ad torn from an old magazine at Aunt Emma's house. The magnificent dollhouse on the page was a beauty to behold. One view showed the front of the house with its columned porch, windows of real glass that opened and closed, a tiled roof, and two chimneys.

Another view displayed the inside of the house, seven rooms filled with fancy furniture and a family of tiny dolls. Why, such a treasure could provide hours—no, years—of fun!

Sarah Beth had not asked for the dollhouse last Christmas. She knew that her parents couldn't afford such a gift, and she hadn't wanted to make them feel bad. She hadn't asked for the stove either. It was a surprise gift—totally unexpected and totally delightful. Mama must have noticed Sarah Beth lingering over the stove in the Woolworth store downtown. Figuring out a way to pay for it, Mama and Daddy had gone back to buy it.

Sarah Beth wondered what her mama had given up in order to buy the stove. Mama was like that. She went without things she really needed in order to make her children happy.

The stove was a marvelous thing, electric just like Aunt Emma's cookstove, only smaller. Of course, Sarah Beth couldn't hook up the toy stove at home because their house wasn't wired for electricity. But one day she took the stove to Aunt Emma's house, and she and Aunt Emma fried some thin bits of potato on the toy stove and baked a tiny cake in its oven.

Sarah Beth ate the potatoes, but she took the cake home and kept it for weeks. She used it for tea parties with her dolls until it was completely covered with mold and Mama insisted that she throw it out.

Sarah Beth looked at the dollhouse in the ad again. The house, the furniture, and the small dolls were sold separately. She checked the price of each. It was a lot of money. If she added the money from the chickens to the coins she had been saving, could she possibly buy the house and some furniture? She'd have to do some figuring. Right now her savings jar contained mostly pennies. There were very few nickels and dimes.

Sarah Beth's daydreaming was interrupted by Mama's announcement that it was bedtime. The family gathered for their nightly Bible story and prayers. Then it was off to bed for everyone.

As the children walked to school the next morning, Sarah Beth asked Lynwood how much money twenty-four fryers would bring. He had raised a brood of chickens for two years. Now he was raising rabbits.

"I don't know what the price of fryers is right now, let alone what it will be in the fall," Lynwood replied. "It's way too soon to answer that question."

He sounds just like Grandma, Sarah Beth thought.

"But how much did your fryers weigh last fall?" Sarah Beth asked persistently.

"I think they averaged about three pounds each." Lynwood tried to recall. "Some weighed a little more, some a little less."

Half a mile down the road, the children were joined by Jesse and Mary Adams. Their conversation turned to other things as they walked the remaining half mile to school.

The school was a three-room brick building. Children in the first three grades were all in one room. The fourth and fifth graders were in Sarah Beth's room. Lynwood was in the seventh grade. The sixth graders were also in his room.

Sarah Beth and Lynwood's mama sometimes told them stories about her school days. She had gone to school on this same spot, but her school building had had only two rooms. One room was stacked on top of the other in a white wooden building. That white schoolhouse had been torn down when the present brick one was built.

School would soon be out for the summer, and Mrs. Davis was spending a lot of time helping her pupils prepare for exams. Students with good attendance records and an A-average in a subject did not have to take the exam in that subject. Sarah Beth was totally exempt from exams. She didn't have to take an exam in any subject.

While other pupils reviewed for exams, those who were exempt had time for reading or for helping classmates review the materials covered during the year. For a while Sarah Beth helped her friend Mary review some arithmetic problems. Sarah Beth was good at solving the story problems in the arithmetic book, even though she couldn't see why anyone would ever need to solve some of those problems.

When Mrs. Davis called Mary to a group that was reviewing history, Sarah Beth went back to her own desk and took out her tablet. She never wasted paper, but surely it wouldn't be a waste to use one sheet to solve a real-life problem.

First, she wrote down the question to be answered—just like Mrs. Davis had taught them to do in arithmetic class.

Can I earn enough money from the sale of 24 chickens to buy a dollhouse, some furniture, and some dolls?

Next, Sarah Beth wrote down the known facts.

| | |
|---|---|
| Dollhouse | $ 8.50 |
| Furniture | $ 2.25 |
| Small dolls | $ 1.50 |
| TOTAL NEEDED | $12.25 |

Sarah Beth added the first three figures and wrote down the total. That was how much money she needed. Next, she wrote down some other facts.

3 lbs. per fryer × $_____ per lb. = $_____ per fryer
24 fryers × $_____ per fryer = $_____

Right now there were too many unknown facts to solve this problem. Sarah Beth would have to find those facts.

After school Lynwood and Sarah Beth stopped at the little store at the crossroads, catty-cornered from the school. Sarah Beth bought a tablet and some pencils. She handed Mr. McDaniels a dime, and he gave her two pennies in change. When the change was no more than two cents, Lynwood and Sarah Beth were allowed to spend it.

Sarah Beth looked at the candy in the glass case. She always had a hard time deciding between a Tootsie Roll and a Mary Jane candy. Today she could buy both; or she could buy one and save a penny. Instead, she decided to save both pennies.

While Lynwood was looking at all the candies in the case, Sarah Beth asked the storekeeper, "What's the price per pound for dressed fryers?"

"Right now they're bringing 27 cents a pound because there aren't many frying chickens for sale at this time of year," Mr. McDaniels answered. "Who knows what the price will be next week—or even tomorrow?" What a strange question for a child to ask at this time of year, he thought.

Sarah Beth filed the answer away in her head. Now she had one more fact for her arithmetic problem.

When the children got home from school, Sarah Beth went to her room to change clothes. There was a book on her bed. It was an old book, but it was still beautiful. The cover was leather, and the title was printed in magnificent gold letters: *Aesop's Fables*. She had read a fable by Aesop in her reader at school, but she had never seen this book. She opened the book's cover, and there in a neat handwriting were the words: *To Sarah Wright, my brave and devoted daughter, from your loving mother, September 16, 1876.*

Why, that was Grandma's name before she was married! Sarah Beth had been named for both her grandmothers. This must be one of the treasures Grandma saved when they had the sale after Grandpa died.

Grandma had a trunk in her room. Once when Sarah Beth had asked what was in the trunk, Grandma told her about the sale. In the trunk were a few items that Grandma couldn't bear to sell.

Sarah Beth looked again at the date of the inscription. Why, Grandma was just a girl—not much older than I am now when she was given this book, Sarah Beth thought. In the book was a book-mark, one that Sarah Beth had made for Grandma. Sarah Beth was curious and turned to the marked passage.

The title of the fable on the page was "The Milkmaid and Her Pail." Sarah Beth had never read this story. It was about a girl carrying a pail of milk and daydreaming. She dreamed about making and selling butter, buying eggs to hatch, and selling chickens to get money for a fine new gown. While dreaming about the party to which she would wear the fine gown, the maid tripped and spilled all the milk. The moral of the story was printed in big bold black letters: **Do not count your chickens before they are hatched.**

Sarah Beth had a general idea about why Grandma had put the book on her bed. But what exactly was Grandma trying to tell her? Was it wrong to try to earn money for something you really wanted? Did Grandma think Sarah Beth was too careless to raise chickens?

Sarah Beth wanted to ask Grandma about the beautiful book. For what occasion did Grandma receive the gift? Her birthday wasn't in September. And what had Grandma done to deserve being called *brave*? Sarah Beth wanted to know the story behind the book, but she was not so sure she wanted to discuss the fable about the milkmaid with Grandma.

She took the beautiful book to Grandma's room and carefully placed it on the high chest of drawers so that Will could not reach it if he toddled into the room.

∞

For the next two days, Sarah Beth checked the old Dominicker before and after school and again just before dark. Each time she looked, the hen was sitting on the nest. When Sarah Beth scattered grain for the hens, the Dominicker flew to the floor, hastily ate a few grains, and then returned to the nest. She stayed on the nest at night, too, instead of roosting with the other hens. No doubt about it. This was a settin' hen.

Mama helped Sarah Beth choose eggs to place under the hen. Some of the eggs were white ones from the Leghorns in the flock; others were brown eggs from the Rhode Island Reds and Dominickers. Sarah Beth was glad there were more brown eggs than white eggs. Brown eggs meant bigger chickens; and bigger chickens meant more money when they were sold as fryers.

Mama lifted the hen to the floor. She and Sarah Beth put twenty-four eggs into the nest and then carefully placed the hen on the eggs.

With her beak, the Dominicker pushed some uncovered eggs under her warm body. She clucked softly. "She'll be a good mother hen," said Sarah Beth.

11

Mama and Sarah Beth watched the hen for a few minutes. The hen was having a hard time keeping all the eggs covered. "We'd better take a couple of eggs out," said Mama. "If we don't, some of the eggs will not be kept warm and won't hatch." Reluctantly Sarah Beth agreed.

On the big calendar in the kitchen, in the space under May 15, Sarah Beth wrote *Set hen*. She counted off the twenty-one days it would take for the eggs to hatch and made a big red circle around June 5.

Then she went to her room and took out the piece of paper on which she had stated her problem. She crossed out the *24* in front of *fryers* and wrote *22*. Old Dominicker could hatch only twenty-two baby chicks.

∽

On Sunday morning Sarah Beth checked the hen house before she went to church. She wanted to make sure Old Dominicker was keeping all the eggs covered. The hen was doing her job well. Not one egg peeked from under her speckled feathers.

In Sunday school that day, Miss Lily told a story from Genesis 28 about Jacob and his dream about a ladder going up to heaven. In the story God promised to give Jacob land and to care for him and his family. Jacob made a promise, too. He said to God, "Of all that thou shalt give me I will surely give the tenth unto thee." Miss Lily said this was called tithing.

Then the teacher gave each pupil a Bible reference to find and read aloud. Each verse was about giving a tithe or an offering to God. Sarah Beth's verse was Leviticus 27:32.

*And concerning the tithe of the herd, or of the flock, even of whatsoever passeth under the rod, the tenth shall be holy unto the Lord.*

Miss Lily had a way of making the meaning of scriptures clear. She described how a shepherd counted herds of cattle or flocks of

12

sheep. When the animals entered a pen, the shepherd put his rod across the gate. As the animals passed under the rod one at a time, he counted them. Miss Lily didn't say anything about chickens, but Sarah Beth imagined that "whatsoever" might include chickens.

Sarah Beth knew that Mama and Daddy tithed. They gave to the church one-tenth of every dollar Daddy earned at the bakery and one-tenth of every dollar they got from selling eggs and butter and vegetables.

Sarah Beth had never had any money to tithe. Daddy gave her and her brothers money to put in the offering at Sunday school and worship. He gave them money to buy school supplies, too. There was a penny or two left over sometimes, but you couldn't give a tithe of one penny, or even two pennies.

Sarah Beth reckoned she would be expected to tithe the money she would earn from her chickens. One-tenth of twenty-two chickens would be two and two-tenths chickens. In arithmetic class she was taught to round off numbers in division. God would probably be satisfied with two chickens. Two of the white Leghorns would be God's chickens, she decided.

Miss Lily had once said that no one knows what God looks like, that God is spirit. We can feel that he is near or hear his voice in our hearts, but we can't see him. But Sarah Beth had seen a picture of God in a Bible story book. He had a long white beard. He wore a long white gown. He was surrounded by piles of puffy white clouds. No doubt about it. Two white Leghorns were definitely the chickens for God—even if they would be smaller and bring a little less money.

# CHAPTER 2

# Money for Chores?

It was a rainy day. When the children came home from school, Grandma had the quilt box in the living room. "It's too wet to do anything outside," she said to Sarah Beth. "I thought this would be a good time to get back to your quilt."

Last winter Grandma had insisted that every nine-year-old girl should make a quilt. So Sarah Beth started making nine-diamond quilt squares, because Grandma said this was the easiest pattern for a beginner.

They had cut dozens of three-inch squares of fabric, stacking the dark pieces in one pile and the light ones in another.

In the beginning, as they started sewing the tiny pieces together, Sarah Beth had asked whether the quilt wouldn't be just as warm if they sewed big pieces together.

"Most of the pieces we use are left over from making dresses or other clothing. There usually aren't very many large pieces left over," Grandma had explained. "Sewing the small scraps into a quilt is one way to avoid waste. Besides, the small pieces make a beautiful quilt."

Sarah Beth surely couldn't argue with that. Many of the quilts Grandma and Mama had sewn contained intricate designs that were indeed beautiful.

Sarah Beth looked at some of the squares she had already made. It was fun to recall the sources of some of the pieces: dark calico pieces with small flowers from Grandma's dresses; more vibrant colors and bolder prints from Mama's dresses; tiny blue checks from Will's rompers; some solid pieces from shirts. Sarah Beth admired one square with a pale purple print from the fabric of her own favorite dress.

"When I am as old as you, Grandma, and look at this quilt, will I remember that I had a dress like this?" she asked.

"Perhaps," Grandma answered, "if you don't wear out the quilt long before you are that old."

Sarah Beth began to sew. When she had sewn three pieces together in a row, Grandma picked up the strip and looked at it.

"Your stitches are fairly even," Grandma said. "Just try to make them a little smaller on the next row."

Sarah Beth was relieved. If I live to be a hundred years old, my stitches will never be as small and even as Grandma's, she thought to herself. At least Grandma didn't ask me to take the stitches out and resew the seam. Sarah Beth wondered how many seams she had resewn when she started making the quilt last winter.

For a short time they sewed in silence. Then Grandma spoke. "Thank you for putting my book on the chest where Will couldn't reach it. I'd hate for anything to happen to that book."

"It's a beautiful book," Sarah Beth interrupted before Grandma could turn the conversation to the fable about the milkmaid. "Why did your mama give you such a fine present? And why did she call you brave?"

"During the summer following my tenth birthday, my mama was very ill," Grandma began. "One day she told me that I could not go back to school in the fall, because I was needed at home to care for her and my younger brothers."

"Mama knew how much school meant to me," Grandma continued, "and how much joy it brought to my life. Even though I never complained, she understood how hard it was for me to give up school. On the day my brothers went back to school, Mama gave me the book of Aesop's fables. It was the last gift my mama gave me. She died a few weeks later."

No wonder the book was so precious to Grandma, Sarah Beth thought. She was quiet for a few moments. Then she asked, "Did you go back to school after your mama died?"

"No, child," Grandma replied, "I had to keep house for my family and raise my younger brothers."

Sarah Beth tried to imagine what it would be like to have to drop out of school and never go back. She didn't think she could do that without complaining. Yes, Grandma had really been brave.

For some reason, which Sarah Beth herself could not explain, she decided to ask Grandma about the fable of the milkmaid that ended with the moral "Do not count your chickens before they are hatched."

"Grandma," she began slowly, "why did you want me to read the story about the milkmaid? Is it wrong to dream about something you want very much and to plan how to get it?"

"Not unless you fix your mind and heart wholly on that one thing and forget other things that may be more important," Grandma replied.

Sarah Beth thought about that before she spoke again. "I want the dollhouse very much," she admitted, "but I'm remembering important things, too. I'm going to give two chickens to God. That's a tithe." She decided not to mention which two chickens would be God's.

"That's an important thing to do," Grandma said. Then she added, "The fable also says something more to me. It says we can't be sure of the future. We can plan carefully and work hard, but sometimes things that are beyond our control can keep us from getting what we want."

It was time to start evening chores. As Sarah Beth helped Grandma put away the sewing, she recalled something beyond her control that had already changed her plans. The hen could not cover as many eggs as Sarah Beth had planned.

∞

A few days later Sarah Beth was reading a mystery story when Mama reminded her that the stairs in the front hall had not been dusted. Of all her chores, Sarah Beth hated this one most. She usually put it off until Mama told her to do it.

Sarah Beth reluctantly laid down her book. She got the feather duster and hastily swished it across each step. She had put away the duster and picked up her book when she again heard Mama's voice.

"Sarah Elizabeth Miller, look at those stairs," Mama said with a frown. When Mama used all three of your names in that tone of voice, you knew she was upset. Mama continued, "You just moved the dust into the corners of the steps. Now get a dustcloth and clean the stairs. And don't forget to dust between the banisters." Mama spoke sternly.

Sarah Beth took the dustcloth and carefully dusted each step, taking pains to go between the banisters and wipe the edge of each step. While she worked, a plan was forming in her mind.

Just before bedtime that evening, Sarah Beth took the first step in her plan. "Mama," she asked, "if I do a good job of cleaning the stairs each week without being reminded, could you give me a nickel for the job?"

To Sarah Beth's surprise, Mama didn't even stop to think before she answered. "No, Sarah Beth," Mama said. "I don't get paid for washing and ironing our clothes. Your daddy doesn't get paid for chopping wood for the stove. Lynwood doesn't get paid for carrying wood into the kitchen. Grandma doesn't get paid for mending our clothes. We all have many chores to do around the house, but we don't get paid for them."

Daddy, who had been listening to the conversation from behind the newspaper, laid the paper down. "Your mama is right," he agreed. "Each of us must do our regular chores without expecting pay. That's what being part of a family means." He waited a moment for that idea to sink into Sarah Beth's mind. Then he added, "Sometimes there are extra tasks to be done. Perhaps you could earn an occasional nickel by helping with one of them."

"Could I really, Daddy? I'll work very hard for a nickel," Sarah Beth said excitedly.

"In fact, there is a special job that needs to be done tomorrow," Daddy explained. "I noticed a lot of bugs on the potato vines. Insect spray is very expensive this year, and I don't much like to use it anyway. I'll pay you and Lynwood if you get rid of those bugs tomorrow. I'll show you how to do it."

The next day was Saturday. Before Daddy left for work, the children joined him in the potato patch. He handed each one an old tin pan into which he had poured some kerosene. "Tap each potato vine gently so the bugs fall into the pan," Daddy explained as he demonstrated the process. "If bugs fall on the ground instead of into the pan, you'll need to pick them up and put them in the pan. Otherwise they'll fly back onto the vine."

Sarah Beth tapped a potato vine over her pan. Several bugs flew into the air.

"Tap the vine a bit more quickly but less vigorously," Daddy said, showing her again how it was to be done.

Before long both children had gotten the hang of the job, and Daddy left for work.

The children moved quickly along the rows. "Ugh! This kerosene stinks," Sarah Beth moaned. "And I hate the feel of those bugs when I have to pick them up from the ground."

"Stop complaining," her brother ordered. "Do you want to earn some money or not?"

"Of course, I do. You know that," Sarah Beth replied crossly.

They worked in silence for a short time. Then Sarah Beth whined, "I feel a bug crawling on the back of my neck. Get it off of me."

Lynwood ignored her.

"PLEASE," she begged.

Exasperated, Lynwood set his pan down and examined his sister's neck. "There's nothing on your neck. You're just imagining it," he said as he picked up his pan and attacked the real bugs on the potato vines.

Then, feeling sorry for his sister, Lynwood suggested, "Why don't you think about what you'll do with the money you earn? Maybe that'll make the job seem a little easier."

Sarah Beth began to dream of the dollhouse in the ad. Suddenly the careless milkmaid of the fable popped into her mind, interrupting her dream. I mustn't get so wrapped up in my dream that I spill the kerosene or miss some of the bugs, she told herself.

She wondered if Lynwood was dreaming of the bicycle he wanted to buy. She asked him, "When all your baby rabbits are big enough to sell, will you have enough money for your bicycle?"

"I might, if Dad and I can find a good used bike," he said hopefully.

Sarah Beth hadn't even thought about the possibility of a used dollhouse. She wasn't sure she could be satisfied with a used one, but she didn't tell Lynwood that.

The children worked diligently. Finally they reached the end of the last two rows of potatoes. Lynwood walked back through the patch to see if he could spy any bugs that had escaped. Now and then he picked off a stray one.

Daddy came home in a happy mood that evening. When he inspected the potato patch and saw what a good job the children had done, he said to them, "Close your eyes and hold out your hand." Into each child's hand he dropped a coin. Sarah Beth opened her eyes and saw not a nickel, not a dime, but a big round quarter. She gave Daddy a big hug.

After supper Daddy went to the car, got a big box out of the trunk, and carried it into the living room.

"Uncle Ben sold the twin calves for me," Daddy said, "and I have a surprise for the family."

From the carton he took out what looked like a thin, rectangular box of polished wood with a design carved into the sides and ends. Then he took out four legs and attached them to the box. What's so wonderful about a box table? Sarah Beth wondered. But she did not express her disappointment. She watched as Daddy lifted a lid in the top of the box. Inside the box he placed some big batteries with wires. Next, Daddy took something else out of the cardboard box and set it on top of the box table.

"A radio!" squealed Lynwood and Sarah Beth. It looked almost like the electric radios in the homes of many of their friends and neighbors.

"We still can't afford the cost of running an electric line from the main road down the lane to our house," Daddy explained. "But with the money from the extra calf this spring, your mother and I decided we could buy a battery radio."

When Grandma realized that the surprise was a radio, she muttered something about a "worldly contraption" and went upstairs to her room.

Mama didn't say anything, but Sarah Beth noticed a strange look in her mama's eyes. Was it disappointment? or hurt? Sarah Beth couldn't tell. It surely couldn't have been surprise.

Grandma worried a lot about her family becoming too worldly. Sarah Beth hadn't figured out exactly what being worldly meant. It seemed to have something to do with wanting fine things and caring more about what other people thought than about what God wanted and thought.

Grandma still wore long dresses of dark fabric with a matching cape and apron. She also wore a white cap that she covered with a black bonnet when she went outside. She said that plain clothes set one apart from the world.

Grandma's clothes surely were not what you could call fine, thought Sarah Beth. And they certainly did set her apart from the neighbors—and even from most of the church members. What Sarah Beth didn't understand was why these clothes pleased God more than ordinary clothes. Someday she and Grandma would talk about that.

Right now Sarah Beth was so excited about the new radio that she couldn't think about anything else.

After connecting the wires from the batteries to the radio, Daddy turned a knob. A voice filled the room. Will, who was shy around strangers, ran to Mama's side. From behind Mama's skirt he peered around the room, his eyes searching every corner. "Where is man?" he asked, puzzled.

Mama tried to explain that the voice was coming from the box, but it was beyond the little boy's comprehension. Mama picked him up and held him on her lap to reassure him that all was well.

A radio reporter with a pleasant voice was speaking. Daddy said the reporter's name was Lowell Thomas. Mr. Thomas was talking about something he called a depression in America. He described farms that had turned into dust, leaving farmers with no crops. He told about factories that had closed, leaving thousands of people without jobs. He talked about families who had no homes and no food.

It was later than usual when Mama announced bedtime. Still, sleep did not come quickly to Sarah Beth. She lay in the quiet darkness thinking how fortunate she was to have earned twenty-five cents for a few hours of work when many children were hungry because their fathers had no work that day. Maybe she should consider a secondhand dollhouse instead of an expensive new one, she thought.

∞

The schoolhouse was buzzing with excitement. The principal had announced that on the last day of school all seven grades would go to Lakeside, the amusement park. School buses would take the children, and they would bring their lunches and eat there. The PTA would provide lemonade. The pupils were required to bring a note from their parents giving permission for the trip.

The principal said that many parents would be needed to help the teachers supervise the children. Sarah Beth told her teacher that she was sure her mother would volunteer.

As soon as the children got home from school, Lynwood and Sarah Beth told Mama about the trip to Lakeside. Sure enough, she volunteered to go along. The last day of school had already been marked on the calendar weeks ago when the children began counting the number of days remaining in the school year.

Sarah Beth had also marked the day *after* the close of school on the calendar. That was the day her chickens would hatch.

When Daddy got home from work that day, he told Sarah Beth he would help her prepare a coop for her chickens, which would be the first brood to hatch this year.

The coops had been stored during the winter. They chose one and moved it to a sheltered place near the hen house. A loose board and one of the door hinges needed to be repaired, and the inside of the coop had to be cleaned and covered with fresh straw. Daddy said he would make a trough to hold mash for the baby chicks to eat. Sarah Beth thought she could find an old pan to use for water.

Sarah Beth enjoyed working with Daddy. If you wanted to talk with him at this time of year, you had to do it while he was working. Almost all of his waking hours were spent in the garden or barn or woodshed after his day's work at the bakery.

Today Sarah Beth and Daddy talked about the coming school trip, the new radio, and the soon-to-be-hatched chickens.

"How much money do you think I'll get for my chickens?" Sarah Beth asked Daddy.

"It's impossible to answer that question now, Sarah Beth," he replied. "Things are too uncertain in our country. Lots of workers have lost their jobs. Others don't know if they'll have jobs tomorrow. And when people don't have money to spend, prices are low. We can't predict how much money chickens will bring in the fall. We must live one day at a time and be thankful for the blessings that day brings."

Sarah Beth was quiet. She was thinking about her classmate Norma, whose father had lost his job and couldn't find work to do. Norma didn't have money for school supplies. Sometimes their teacher, Mrs. Davis, gave her paper and pencils.

Daddy continued, "Our family is lucky. We have land on which to raise food. When no rain comes we can irrigate our garden with water from the spring. And I still have a job. While it doesn't pay much, I earn enough to buy the things we really need and to pay back each month a little of the money we have borrowed to pay for our car and house."

"We really are lucky," Sarah Beth agreed.

Then Daddy looked at the coop and pronounced it ready for occupancy by its new family of chicks.

# CHAPTER 3

# Summertime Fun and Duties

The schoolyard—and sometimes even the classrooms —hummed with conversations about the coming trip to the amusement park, about how much money children would bring to spend, about which rides they would enjoy, about who they would sit with on the bus. Since they all walked to school, it would be the first ride on a school bus for most of them.

At last the big day arrived. Two yellow school buses pulled up to the schoolyard. Teachers and parents lined the children up two by two and shepherded them onto the buses. Sarah Beth and her friend Mary sat together. After a short ride, they all arrived at the park.

Daddy had given Lynwood and Sarah Beth each twenty-five cents. Tickets for the rides and amusements cost five cents each. Soft drinks, cotton candy, ice cream, and other treats also could be purchased in the park.

Sarah Beth watched as Lynwood and his friends headed for the roller coaster called the Thriller. It was the biggest roller coaster in the state. She liked to watch the open cars with their dips and rolls and screaming riders, but she had no desire to try it herself.

Sarah Beth and Mary rode the bumper cars and the airplanes. Sarah Beth wondered what it would be like to ride in a real airplane instead of ones that were fastened to a center pole and flew around in circles.

Mary wanted to go through the Crazy House, but Sarah Beth wasn't too keen on that. She much preferred to ride the ferris wheel and look out over the whole park. But she gave in to her friend's pleas.

The girls giggled at themselves in the funny mirrors that transformed them into all kinds of strange and grotesque shapes and sizes. But when they entered the thick darkness of the haunted tunnel with its weird noises and hands that reached out and grabbed them, they shrieked and held onto one another. Sarah Beth was relieved when, at last, they came into a dimly lit room and then slid down a slide, out into the bright sunlight.

As the girls passed the hobby horses, Mary's little sister waved to them. Although fourth graders were much too big for this ride, Sarah Beth enjoyed watching the beautiful horses go up and down as the carousel turned.

When Mary suggested that they ride the Whip next, Sarah Beth hesitated. She had only two nickels left. She wanted to save one for pink cotton candy, and she thought a cold Grape Nehi soft drink would taste better than lemonade with the lunch she had brought.

She was saved from making an immediate decision when two of their classmates called out, "There's room for one more in this car on the Whip. One of you come on so the ride can begin." At Sarah Beth's urging, Mary joined the other girls.

Sarah Beth watched the revolving cars whip the riders first in one direction and then another. Then she decided to walk over to the live pony rides and say hello to Charlie, one of the ponies.

In the winter when the park was closed, Charlie stayed on Uncle Ben's farm. There Sarah Beth rode him as often as she wished. Now a small boy was riding Charlie around a circular path. When the ride ended, the man in charge of the pony rides let Sarah Beth pet Charlie. She felt sure the pony recognized her. She wished she had a lump of sugar to give him.

When Sarah Beth went back to the Whip to join her friends, she heard the loud ring of the principal's big bell. This was the signal that all the children were to gather at the picnic site for lunch.

On the way, the girls walked past the large swimming pool. They stopped to watch some big boys dive from the high boards into the greenish-blue water at the deep end of the pool.

Sarah Beth noticed Norma Gibson and her older sister, Helen, sitting on a bench near the fence that separated the pool from the rest of the park. Sarah Beth guessed that the girls had spent the morning watching the swimmers because they had no money for rides.

"It's fun to watch the swimmers," Sarah Beth said to Norma, "but it's time for lunch now. Didn't you hear the bell ring?"

"In the excitement this morning, we forgot our lunches," Helen explained quickly. "We'll just watch the swimmers now and eat when we get home."

Sarah Beth remembered that Norma was among the fourth-graders who had permission to go home for lunch every day. Was it possible that she went home because her mother didn't have enough food to pack lunches? Sarah Beth wondered.

"Mama says a few lunches are always forgotten or lost," Sarah Beth said, "so she packed extra sandwiches. So did some other mothers. We'll share with you. Mama also brought some of my grandma's sugar cookies and a basket of sweet cherries from the tree at the end of our garden."

Helen hesitated, but when she saw how eager Norma looked, she agreed to join the picnickers.

The teachers and parents helped all the children find the lunches they had brought from home. When Sarah Beth explained that Helen and Norma had forgotten their lunches, Sarah Beth's mama invited them over to share sandwiches. She laid out egg salad sand-wiches, jelly sandwiches, and sandwiches made with raisins and carrots in a homemade dressing. All the sandwiches were made of real sandwich bread from the bakery. Mama also divided up the cookies and cherries, asking Sarah Beth to take some to Lynwood, who had taken his lunch poke and joined some of his classmates.

After everyone was seated on the grass, the principal asked them all to bow their heads while she thanked God for the food.

Sarah Beth noticed that Norma wolfed her sandwiches down hungrily, while Helen took tiny bites and chewed slowly as if savor-ing every delicious crumb.

Sarah Beth had changed her mind about the Grape Nehi. Instead, she took a cup of the PTA lemonade. She considered buy-ing cotton candy for herself with one nickel and another cotton candy for Norma and Helen to share. Then she had a better idea.

Sarah Beth went over to where her mama was sitting with some other parents. "Do you have a nickel I can borrow?" she whispered to her mama. "When we get home, I'll pay it back with a nickel from my savings jar." She explained why she wanted the money now.

Mama rummaged through her pocketbook, pulled out a coin, and handed it to Sarah Beth. When the teachers gave permission for the children to go to the refreshment stands, Sarah Beth slipped a nickel into Norma's hand and another into Helen's hand. Sarah Beth had decided to let the two sisters choose what to buy. "Get anything you want," she whispered.

Sarah Beth and Mary bought cotton candy. Helen and Norma waited in another line. When both girls bought milk, Sarah Beth was amazed. Not even chocolate milk. Just plain ordinary white milk, mind you. And what's more, they didn't even drink one swallow of the milk. They put it in a brown poke.

For a while the children enjoyed their treats from the refreshment stand and talked and played in the grassy picnic area. All too soon, it was time to get on the buses and return to school. There, friends bid each other and their teachers goodbye for the summer.

When they returned home, Sarah Beth and Lynwood told Grandma and Will all about the wonderful day at the park. Then Sarah Beth went upstairs, took a nickel from her savings jar, and subtracted five cents from her record of how much money was in the jar.

Sarah Beth took the nickel to Mama. "I told Norma and Helen to have a nice treat, but they didn't," she complained. Sarah Beth explained about the plain white milk the girls bought and put in a poke.

Mama wasn't surprised. "I talked to Mrs. Davis," Mama said. "The Gibson family has two small children at home. I suspect the milk was for them." Mama went on to explain that the Gibson family had lost their home and moved in with relatives just outside the city. They had no money to buy the kind of food the children needed. Mama planned to talk to the deacons at church about how they might help the family.

When Sarah Beth realized how concerned Mama was for Norma and Helen, she almost wished Mama would give her nickel back.

But Mama didn't do that. She gave Sarah Beth a warm hug. "I'm very proud of you for sharing with the girls," she said fondly.

Sarah Beth stole a glance at Grandma, who had been listening to the conversation. Grandma was forever saying that we shouldn't be proud of anything. To hear her tell it, being proud was a great sin, right up there—or maybe down there—with being worldly. She was always lamenting that pride and worldliness were infecting the church.

Sometimes Sarah Beth thought that Grandma was proud of not being proud—if such a thing were possible. Sarah Beth didn't really know about that. But she knew that Mama's hug and words of praise had made her feel warm and loved.

Sarah Beth went back to her room, changed her clothes, and hurried to the chicken house. When she approached Old Dominicker's nest, she heard a faint peep. One baby chick had hatched! And several others were partially out of the eggs. Most of the eggs had cracks where the chicks inside were pecking at the shells and trying to emerge.

Sarah Beth fairly flew to the house to share the good news. How could one day bring so much joy? The splendid trip to Lakeside, the welcome beginning of summer vacation, Mama's warm words of praise, and now the exciting discovery that tomorrow she would have a brood of chickens of her very own.

∞

The next morning Sarah Beth heard a rooster crow. The sun had not yet peeked above the eastern mountains. She lay still, listening for any sound of motion in the house. All was quiet. No one was up and about.

Sarah Beth was too excited to go back to sleep. Without making a sound, she slipped into her clothes. She crept down the stairs, avoiding the worn center of each step so that it would not creak under the weight of her footstep. She managed to open both the door and screen door without one tiny squeak. She gingerly closed the screen door, leaving the other door open.

Once outside she raced to the hen house and went inside. Ignoring Old Dominicker's protests and pecks, she lifted the hen off the nest. The nest was filled with soft, cuddly chicks, ranging in color from pale yellow to reddish brown to black. She counted. "One, two, three…." There were twenty chicks in the nest. Picking the shell fragments from the straw, she found two unhatched eggs. She carefully replaced the hen on the nest. The two remaining eggs must be kept warm until they hatched.

Sarah Beth decided to feed the hens before returning to the house. Then that chore would be out of the way. She went to the feed house, took some grain from a sack, and scattered it for the hens. She also filled their water pans.

When Sarah Beth got back to the house, Mama was cooking breakfast, and Grandma was setting the table. Daddy and Lynwood had gone to the barn to milk Blossom and Josephine and to feed the other animals.

Bubbling with enthusiasm, Sarah Beth shared the wonderful news of the nest full of beautiful chicks. "Maybe the other two eggs are hatching at this very minute," she suggested hopefully.

When Daddy and Lynwood returned from their chores in the barn and Will was awake, Sarah Beth repeated her good news. Will wanted to see the baby chicks right away, but Mama said, "Not until after breakfast."

When the family had finished eating, Sarah Beth led Mama and Will out to see the chickens. The mother hen had flown from the nest and stood on the floor, scratching in the straw and clucking to her babies. "The hen wants the chicks to join her," Mama said.

Then Mama examined the two eggs in the nest. "They are not going to hatch," she told Sarah Beth.

"Can't we wait one more day to be sure?" Sarah Beth begged.

"Look at that hen," Mama answered. "She knows her setting days are over. There's no way you're going to get her to stay on the nest any longer."

Sarah Beth's face clouded over with disappointment. Although she knew that some eggs in a setting often failed to hatch, she had been counting on twenty-two chickens ever since they put the eggs under the hen. Now she would have to revise the facts in her problem again. Sarah Beth took a last look at the eggs that didn't hatch. One of them was white. Maybe one of God's white Leghorns had failed to hatch.

The little chicks were so beautiful and lively that the sight of them dissolved the cloud on Sarah Beth's face, and she was filled with delight and anticipation.

Mama picked up the hen and held the complaining Dominicker while Sarah Beth got a basket and carried the baby chicks to the waiting coop. When all the babies were inside the coop, Mama carefully placed the hen at the door of the coop.

Sarah Beth, Mama, and Will watched the proud mother hen join the baby chicks, all the while clucking to them softly.

After returning to the house, Sarah Beth took some stale bread from the bread box and crumbled it into small pieces. Then she drew a bucket of water. Will went with her to feed and water the new brood of chicks. She filled the water pan outside the coop. She scattered the bread crumbs on the hard ground. Before long, the hen came out of the coop, clucking to call the chicks to her. When the chicks were outside, the hen scratched the crumbs and began to pick them up with her beak. Soon the baby chicks began to follow her example, snatching the bits of bread from the ground and swallowing them greedily.

Will was fascinated by the new babies, but when he bent over to pick one up, Old Dominicker rushed at him angrily. He dropped the chick and jumped back just in time to avoid the protective hen's attack. Using a stick to fend off the hen, Sarah Beth picked up a chick and let her little brother hold the fluffy baby for a short time. But he was careful to stand behind his sister while he petted the chick.

Sarah Beth could have admired the chicks all day long, but she knew she better not neglect her other chores. Reluctantly, she pulled Will away from the chickens and led him back to the house. She joined Mama and Grandma who were shelling peas to can for eating next winter.

As Sarah Beth broke open the pods and removed the small green peas, she thought about the chicks—her very own chickens to raise and to sell, twenty of them. It would be her responsibility to care for them. That meant feeding and watering them twice a day—three times a day while they were small. It meant making sure they were all in the coop with the door securely fastened before dark.

It meant being sure they were sheltered in the coop during storms or heavy rains. You couldn't always depend on a hen to bring her baby chicks in out of the rain. You had to be alert for coming storms, find the chicks, and chase them to the safety of the coop.

Sarah Beth remembered one time when a hen and chicks were left out during a storm. Although the hen had tried to cover her brood with her wings, several of them had crept out and drowned.

Several times that day Sarah Beth went out to check on her chicks. She kept the water pan filled. She put mash in the trough that Daddy had made and watched the chicks learn to eat it. She made sure they didn't stray too far from the coop. Before dark she chased them into the coop and carefully fastened the door.

That night before Sarah Beth went to bed, she got out her notes. She crossed out the *22* for the number of chickens and wrote in *20*. It was the second time she had changed that number. Mama had given her twenty-four eggs. The hen could only cover twenty-two. Only twenty had hatched. She would take extra good care of those twenty.

And that is just what she did. As the days passed, she tended the chickens diligently, caring for their every need.

Old Dominicker proved to be a good mother, watching over her chicks and calling back to her side any that strayed. Usually she led them back to the coop before dark. Sarah Beth counted each chick as it followed the mother hen into the coop.

∽

Summer was a busy time for the Miller family. The garden had to be weeded, hoed or plowed, and watered. When one crop was harvested, another was planted. Vegetables, berries, peaches, plums, apples, and grapes were dried, canned, pickled, or made into jelly. Everyone helped so the family would have food for the winter. Of course, all the regular chores had to be done, too: feeding the animals, milking the cows, churning butter, cooking, cleaning, washing and ironing, chopping wood, and many other jobs.

Even with all the work, there was still time for visiting and having fun. One evening after supper, Jesse and Mary, who lived at the top of the hill, and Edith, Sam, Rachel, and Bessie, who lived at the bottom of the hill, came to play at the Miller home in the middle.

The younger children, Will, Rachel, and Bessie, played with blocks of different sizes and shapes, which Daddy had sawed and sanded until they were smooth. He had made some of them when Lynwood was little and added others over the years. The little children stacked the blocks, loaded them into the wagon, hauled them around, and then unloaded them. They built houses and sheds and trains.

The older children played croquet. Sarah Beth was glad they decided to play partners, because she was not real good at this game. But Sam, her partner, was very good. They would have a shot at winning. As it turned out, however, Jesse and Edith won the game.

"At least we didn't come in last," Sarah Beth said to Sam, as she glanced teasingly at Lynwood and Mary.

After the croquet game, the children played Red Light and, after that, Kick the Can.

While the children played, Daddy, Mama, and Grandma sat on the front porch—Daddy with the newspaper and Mama with a magazine, as Grandma rocked in the rocking chair.

When the neighbor children went home, Lynwood, Sarah Beth, and Will joined the rest of their family on the porch. Sitting in the swing with the older children always made Will feel important. "Higher, higher," he called again and again.

The sun slowly sank behind Fort Lewis Mountain, unfurling layers of rippling ribbon across the sky, creating a crimson sunset fringed with gold and gradually fading to pale pink. The friendly chirping of crickets punctuated the evening stillness, and lightning bugs began to twinkle in the twilight.

To help Will catch lightning bugs, Sarah Beth went into the house for a jar to hold them. As she stepped across the threshold, the darkness of the house stabbed her memory. "Oh, no," she sobbed. "I haven't shut my chickens in the coop."

She had so enjoyed the games with her friends and the enchanting beauty of nightfall that she completely forgot the chickens. What if one of the farm cats or a weasel had entered the coop and stolen some of the chickens? It was the first time she had failed in her responsibilities of caring for the brood.

Sarah Beth felt her way into the kitchen, found a flashlight, and hurried to the chicken coop. Shining the light into the coop, she saw Old Dominicker resting quietly, her wings spread protectively over the chicks. Sarah Beth wondered if she should move the hen and count the chicks. She decided not to disturb them. Instead, she flashed the light all around the area surrounding the coop, searching for any chick that might not have followed the hen into the coop. There was no sign of a stray.

Sarah Beth went back to the house, filled with relief and remorse —relief that the chicks seemed to be safe and secure, remorse that she had neglected to shut them in before dark. How could she have been so irresponsible and forgetful? Would Grandma think she had been careless like the milkmaid in the fable? She vowed never to forget her responsibilities again.

# CHAPTER 4

# A Sudden Storm

Everyone was busy. Mama was making beet pickles. Lynwood filled the wood box and walked out to the county road to get the mail. Will was playing with some pans and a big wooden spoon. Sarah Beth was churning the rich cream that Grandma had poured into the churn.

It didn't require much thought to churn cream into butter. All you had to do was turn the handle that turned the paddle inside the churn. So Sarah Beth thought about her chickens.

They were growing fast. Feathers were replacing the fuzzy down that covered their bodies. And they ate more every day. How much mash would they eat before they were ready to sell? she wondered. When the chickens were sold, would she be expected to pay Daddy for the feed he had bought for them? That was a possibility she had not yet considered. It could mean serious revisions in the arithmetic problem she had written in her tablet.

Grandma was ripping out seams in feed sacks and matching sacks that were alike. One company sold feed for farm animals in sacks made of cotton cloth printed with various designs and colors. These could be made into dish towels, aprons, pajamas, even shirts and dresses. Men looked for matching prints when they bought feed. Women traded sacks with each other to get enough of one kind to make a garment.

"That's a pretty sack," Sarah Beth said, pointing to one that Grandma was folding. "Maybe we can get enough like that to make me a new dress for school this fall."

Interrupting them, Lynwood rushed into the kitchen, waving a letter excitedly. "Look!" he shouted. "A letter from Uncle Tom." He handed it to Grandma.

Uncle Tom had left home in early March after graduating from high school the year before, but he had not been able to find a job. With a few clothes and a little money, he had set out for the North, hoping to find factory work in a big city.

There had been two post cards before this, one from Chicago and one from St. Louis. But neither card reported success in finding work. Many weeks had passed since the family had received the last postcard.

"It has a Texas address," Grandma said as she nervously opened the envelope. When she unfolded the letter, three dollar bills fell out. She tucked them in her apron pocket and began to read the long letter aloud. Uncle Tom wrote that he had run out of money soon after he left home. He had traveled by freight car, sneaking into a car by night and jumping from the slow-moving train before it came into a city where police would search the cars for hoboes.

Dozens of people were traveling this way, Uncle Tom wrote. He had made one good friend, and they had stuck together. When they got off the freight train, they would search for edible food in garbage cans outside restaurants or grocery stores. Sometimes they stopped at farm houses where they were given food in exchange for a day's work.

In mid-May they got off a train near a small Texas town and walked for miles before stopping at a ranch house where they were given a good meal and jobs. The work was hard, but the rancher provided housing and a small salary for his workers. Uncle Tom missed his family very much and sent his love to each one of them.

Finishing the letter, Grandma pulled the dollar bills from her apron pocket. One of the bills was for Grandma. The other two were to be divided among the children: a dollar for Lynwood, seventy-five cents for Sarah Beth, and a quarter for Will. For a brief moment, Sarah Beth had dared to hope that there was a dollar for each child. But she reckoned it was nice for Grandma to have a little money of her very own, too. There must be something that Grandma would like to have.

Mama and Grandma were relieved that Uncle Tom had survived the dangerous travels and had found work. The children were excited about their uncle's adventures.

"Is Uncle Tom a hobo like the one who stopped here a few weeks ago?" Sarah Beth wanted to know. She remembered a man who had asked for food. They had given him supper and breakfast and let him sleep overnight in the barn. He split a big stack of logs before he left, taking with him an old hen and a sack of potatoes Grandma had given him.

Some of the neighbors declared it wasn't safe to let a hobo sleep in the barn. Daddy said he couldn't be certain it was safe, but he knew for sure it was Christian. He reckoned maybe it hadn't been safe for the Good Samaritan to help a stranger on the Jericho Road either.

"Maybe a family in another part of the country was feeding Uncle Tom at the same time we were helping the hobo here," Sarah Beth suggested.

"Uncle Tom's not a hobo now," Lynwood asserted. "He's working on a ranch in Texas. That means he's a cowboy!"

"Is he really a cowboy, Mama?" Sarah Beth asked.

Their conversation was suddenly interrupted. A bolt of lightning zigzagged across the rapidly darkening sky, filling the kitchen with bright light. A boom of thunder followed. Will darted to Mama and grabbed her skirt.

"My chickens!" cried Sarah Beth, racing toward the door.

"I'll help you," volunteered Lynwood, following his sister.

"NO!" Mama commanded. Her tone of voice made both children stop dead in their tracks. "Better to lose chickens than children," Mama declared firmly. "It's too dangerous for you to go outside now." No amount of protesting could change her mind.

Grandma and Mama stopped their work and gathered all the children in the corner of the living room farthest from the windows and fireplace. Sarah Beth prayed that Old Dominicker had gathered her children in a safe place, too."

It was one of those rare summer storms that suddenly comes out of nowhere without warning. One minute the sun was shining; the next minute rain was falling in torrents from the black clouds. Lightning and thunder filled the sky in all directions.

Will sat on Mama's lap and buried his head against her shoulder. Sarah Beth was afraid, too—not for her own safety, but for the lives of her chickens.

Sensing his sister's worry, Lynwood speculated that this kind of sudden storm usually did not last long. He was right. As quickly as it had begun, the lightning ceased, and the rain drizzled to a stop.

As Sarah Beth and Lynwood left the house, the sun burst forth, arching a rainbow across the sky. Sarah Beth hoped that was a good omen. Water still dripped from the trees and rushed in rivulets across the yard and pasture.

The children checked the chicken coop first. It was empty. They were not surprised, since the storm had begun so suddenly and ferociously. They separated, each going in a different direction and searching in widening circles.

Sarah Beth spotted the chickens first and called to her brother. Under some bushes, near a little depression in the ground, Old Dominicker clucked mournfully. A few soaked chickens stood nearby. The motionless bodies of others were scattered about on the ground.

Apparently the hen had tried to protect her chicks by covering them with her wings in the hollowed out place. But she was no longer able to cover all of the growing chicks. Lynwood thought that the force of the rushing water might have flooded the low place and washed some of the chickens from under the hen.

"Almost half my chickens are dead," sobbed Sarah Beth.

"Maybe not," consoled Lynwood, remembering another year when a brood of chickens was caught in a storm. Laying his hand on one of the chicks, he discovered a faint heartbeat. "Run fast to the house and get a box," he ordered.

By the time Sarah Beth returned with the box, Lynwood had gathered the motionless chicks together. Carefully the children placed them in the box and hurried back to the house, leaving Old Dominicker to care for the chicks that were still on their feet.

When Grandma saw the chicks, she opened the door of the oven. It was warm but not hot inside. She found a piece of worn-out blanket and loosely wrapped the limp, soggy bodies in it. Then she placed the box in the oven, leaving the door ajar. Grandma put one stick of wood into the stove to keep the oven just slightly warm.

Sarah Beth watched the chickens anxiously. After a while, she detected a slight motion under the blanket, followed by a faint cheep. Other cheeps soon followed, and chicks began to scratch their way out from under the blanket. Before long, the box was filled with chicks looking none the worse for their experience. Only one chick failed to revive. Sarah Beth left it in the warm box until Grandma told her that it was dead. Then the children took it outside and buried it under the lilac bush.

That evening when Sarah Beth went to close the door of the coop, the chickens were still outside. All looked dry and healthy. When Sarah Beth put Old Dominicker in the coop, the hen coaxed the chickens to come inside. Sarah Beth counted them one by one as they entered.

The tenth chicken to go through the door was white—one of God's chickens, and she recalled the Bible verse from Sunday school: "The tenth shall be holy unto the Lord." She watched the rest of the chickens enter the coop.

Do two chickens still belong to God now that only nineteen are left? Sarah Beth wondered. The one that drowned was not white, she remembered. If you divide nineteen by ten and round off the answer, you still get two. God still has two chickens, she decided.

When Sarah Beth got back to the house, Grandma was still in the kitchen. "Grandma," Sarah Beth said sadly, "I reckon you can't really count your chickens even *after* they're hatched."

39

"We can count them at any given moment," Grandma said. "But we can't count on the number being the same at the end of the summer—or even tomorrow."

During family devotions that night, Daddy asked everyone to name something for which they were thankful. Grandma was thankful that Uncle Tom was safe. Sarah Beth was thankful that Lynwood and Grandma had helped her save most of her chickens. Mama was thankful that her children were safe. Daddy was thankful for the rain that watered the thirsty garden. Sarah Beth felt that was going a bit far. Right now she couldn't really say she was thankful for this particular rain.

Before going to bed, Sarah Beth revised her arithmetic problem once again. The paper was getting messy where she had marked out and changed the number of chickens so many times. Sarah Beth was thankful that the money in her savings jar had grown with the addition of Uncle Tom's gift.

∽

"The iceman comes today," Mama reminded Sarah Beth a few days later. "We'll need extra ice to freeze ice cream. Better order seventy-five pounds."

Sarah Beth chose the sign with a big 75 on it. She placed it in the window facing the road so the man who delivered ice would know how big a block to chip off.

"Tomorrow is the Fourth of July," Sarah Beth told Will, who was following her around. "Daddy will get off work early. We'll have a wienie roast and picnic. Then we'll make homemade ice cream." Her words didn't mean much to Will. He was too young to remember the fun of earlier wienie roasts.

Lynwood and Sarah Beth picked black raspberries for the ice cream, Grandma crushed the berries and ran them through a sieve to remove the seeds, and Mama cooked a soft custard. Then they put the custard and berries in the icebox so they would be cold the next day. Sarah Beth also helped Grandma make a batch of crisp sugar cookies

After a light lunch the next day, everyone helped get ready for the picnic. Grandma made potato salad and lemonade. Mama made deviled eggs and fixed some carrot sticks. Will helped Sarah Beth stack everyday dishes, glasses, and silverware on a tray to be carried outside. Lynwood cut sassafras branches and whittled sharp points on the ends for roasting the wienies.

When Daddy got home, the children helped him make a circle of rocks on the dirt-packed road that led to the barn. In the middle of the circle, Daddy built a fire with logs from the woodshed. Then Mama spread an oilcloth on the grass under a tree nearby, and everyone helped carry out the food.

When it was time to eat, Mama and Daddy and the two older children stuck wienies on the sassafras sticks. Daddy and Lynwood put extra ones on their sticks for Will and Grandma. Then they held the sticks over the embers. The trick was to find a place to stand where the smoke didn't get in their eyes and where the burning logs were hot enough to roast the wienies without burning them. Sarah Beth complained that the smoke kept following her wherever she went.

When the family had enjoyed the other good food and all the wienies they could eat, Mama opened a box of marshmallows. By this time the fire had died down to a few faintly glowing embers, perfect for toasting marshmallows to a golden brown.

Will tried to stuff a handful of the tasty golden puffs into his mouth at one time. He smeared them all over his face, and then tried to stretch his tongue far enough to lick the sticky goo off his cheeks.

"Will looks like a cat washing its face," Lynwood laughed.

When the marshmallows were gone, Daddy and Lynwood put out the fire and joined the others on the grass in the shade for a quiet game of Who Has the Button? Guessing whose hands held the hidden button was Will's favorite game.

After a little rest, Lynwood brought out a baseball and bat. He and Sarah Beth and Daddy played a game of ball, using only one base. While they played, Mama and Grandma carried everything back to the kitchen and put the leftovers into the icebox. Will tagged along, carrying the used napkins and other trash. Then Grandma entertained Will with his favorite books while Sarah Beth and Daddy beat Lynwood and Mama in a game of croquet.

Even on holidays, chores had to be done, but anticipation of what was yet to come made chore time pass swiftly. Finally it was time to make the ice cream. Daddy chipped ice into small slivers. Mama mixed the chilled raspberries and custard and added a pint of rich cream. Then she poured the mixture into the freezer can and inserted the dasher.

The next step was to put the can in the wooden tub, with the dasher held in place by the lid and the handle locked in position. Lynwood poured chipped ice and salt around the gallon can. Daddy and Sarah Beth took turns cranking the handle that turned the dasher and can. At last, the can would barely move when Daddy turned the crank. That meant the ice cream was frozen and ready to eat.

By the time everyone had eaten their fill of sugar cookies and the rich purple ice cream, it was dusk and time for fireworks. Daddy and Lynwood lit several small firecrackers. Then the family sat in the back yard and looked toward the fairgrounds in the distance as the lights of the county fireworks display burst into brilliant patterns against the dark sky.

"What a perfect ending to a wonderful day," Lynwood sighed contentedly.

"Yes, and it's great to enjoy the fireworks from our own yard without worrying about good seats or a parking place," Daddy added. Everyone agreed.

# CHAPTER 5

# Fire!

July weather was hot that summer. The sun blazed fiercely in the early afternoon sky as Sarah Beth sat in the old tire that Daddy had fastened to a tree limb for a swing. Even with the breeze created by her slow swinging, it was hot in the shade.

Mama had gone to her Home Demonstration Club meeting. She had dropped Lynwood off at his friend's home on the way. Will was napping on a quilt spread on the living room floor while Grandma nodded sleepily in a rocking chair nearby.

Sarah Beth wound the chain of the swing tight. She spun dizzily as it unwound. Suddenly she smelled smoke. She sniffed the still air. The smoke seemed to be coming from the direction of the chicken houses. Sure enough, there was a small blaze at one corner of the older chicken house.

Sarah Beth raced to the house and shouted to Grandma, "Fire in the chicken house. Call the fire department!"

Without staying to explain more, Sarah Beth sped to the chicken house. There were hens in one end of the building. In the other end were Lynwood's rabbit hutches, which had been moved there after some dogs had broken into one of them.

Sarah Beth quickly surveyed the situation. Flames licked at the main door of the chicken house. There was no way she could get near that entrance. At the opposite end of the building, there was a small, low door through which chickens could pass.

Sarah Beth darted to that door and opened it. Quickly she got down on her hands and knees and squeezed through the opening. She unlatched and opened the doors to all the rabbit hutches and the door that separated the now squawking hens from the rabbits.

Fed by the straw on the floor of the chicken house, the flames were spreading wildly. In an instant, Sarah Beth realized that she could not possibly move or chase the frightened animals from the building. She could only hope that they would make their way out through the doors she had opened.

Regretfully she swiftly crawled out through the small door she had entered. Gasping for fresh air, she moved to a safe distance. She watched helplessly as the fire devoured the walls and roof, shooting orange flames and billowing clouds of dark smoke into the air.

Sarah Beth prayed that sparks would not reach any other building. She knew that the fire truck would arrive too late to save the already burning building. Once Grandma's message reached the firehouse in the county seat, the fire chief would set out to pick up the volunteer firemen at their places of work throughout the town.

Grandma, carrying Will in her arms, came out to wait with Sarah Beth. Immediately after calling the fire department, she had also sent the call for help over the telephone party line. Soon Uncle Ben arrived with some other neighbors.

With hoses and buckets, the neighbors began to douse the other chicken house, the woodshed, the outhouse, the washhouse, and the smokehouse. At last the fire truck arrived and the fire was quickly extinguished. Thankfully, all the other buildings were safe.

Sarah Beth looked at the sodden ashes—all that remained of the chicken house. Sadly her eyes searched the surrounding area. Two rabbits, one old and one half-grown, crouched in some bushes. A few hens roosted uneasily on a tree branch. All the other rabbits and hens had been burned to ashes.

"Poor Lynwood," Sarah Beth sobbed to Grandma. "How can I tell him that I didn't save his rabbits?"

"No one could possibly have saved them," Grandma said reassuringly, laying a hand on her granddaughter's shoulder.

Everyone wanted to know how the fire started. All Sarah Beth could tell them was where she first spotted the tiny flames. She had no idea how it had started.

When the fire chief examined the area where the fire originated, he discovered the smoked remains of a broken glass jar. "It's possible," he surmised, "that the thick glass focused the sun's rays on nearby straw and kindled sparks. Once ignited, it would have spread rapidly since everything is so dry. But we'll never know for sure," he concluded.

In the excitement of the fire and her concern for the rabbits, Sarah Beth had forgotten her own chickens. Now she saw them far out in the pasture, contentedly eating insects.

After her club meeting, Mama picked up Lynwood and then went to the bakery to pick up Daddy when he got off work.

By the time the three of them arrived home, the firemen and neighbors had all left, but the smell of smoke remained in the still air. The only one unshaken by the gravity of the situation was little Will who excitedly announced, "Fire truck here!" Sarah Beth and Grandma then filled in the details of the fire.

There were tears in Sarah Beth's eyes when she told Lynwood that all but two of his rabbits had burned. "You helped save my chickens, but I didn't save your rabbits," she moaned. What would this do to her brother's hopes of buying a used bicycle? she wondered silently.

It was Daddy who asked the question no one else had thought to ask. "How did the two rabbits and five hens escape from the burning building?"

For the first time, Sarah Beth explained how she had entered the building and opened the door of the hutches and the door that separated the hens and rabbits. "I'm sorry I couldn't chase the rabbits out," she said between sobs.

Mama didn't know whether to scold or praise her daughter for taking such a risk. So she did neither. Proud of her daughter's courage and relieved for her safety, Mama's eyes filled with tears. Without saying a word, and without thinking of her own clean, starched club-meeting-day dress, Mama put her arms around her grimy, sooty daughter and held her close.

Lynwood thanked his sister for her brave efforts to save his rabbits. "Thanks to you, I still have one doe to start over with," he said gratefully.

Daddy and Lynwood did Sarah Beth's chores that evening while Grandma cooked supper. Mama helped Sarah Beth take a bath in the washtub. It took all the warm water from the tank on the cookstove, a kettle of even hotter water, lots of gritty Lava soap, and plenty of scrubbing to wash away the grime and soot.

At suppertime, the family was subdued. Even Will's excitement had dimmed. Sorrow for Lynwood's loss mingled with their gratitude that the fire had been limited to one building. It was Lynwood who directed attention away from the sad events of the day. "We've been so busy talking about the fire that you haven't heard Mama's good news. Tell them, Mama," he said.

Mama shared the news that she had told Lynwood on the way home from the club meeting. The ladies in the club had asked her to represent them at the state convention in Blacksburg in the fall. It was an opportunity to meet people from all over the state and learn about home and farm extension programs provided by the government.

You could tell that Mama was pleased. And so was Daddy. "It's an honor for you to be chosen," Daddy beamed. "You're the youngest homemaker in the club."

Sarah Beth was happy for Mama and proud of her, too. Sarah Beth noticed that even Grandma looked pleased. Not proud, mind you. Just pleased.

That night Sarah Beth was dead tired. Still, sleep was a long time coming. She kept thinking about her brother and his lost rabbits. Lynwood was not like her. He had not cried or complained. Not one bit. He kept all his feelings inside. Still he had to be hurting bad. "Please help me find a way to help Lynwood," she prayed. And then sleep came.

The minute Sarah Beth opened her eyes the next morning she knew exactly how she could help Lynwood. After breakfast she followed him out to the box in which his two surviving rabbits had spent the night.

"You can have half of my chickens," she told her brother. "With the money you'll get from selling them, will you have enough for a bike?" she asked.

"I don't think so," Lynwood said.

"Then maybe you could use the money to buy some more rabbits and start over again," she suggested.

Lynwood looked doubtful. "Replacing the feed and hutches lost in the fire will be expensive," he explained. "Dad said there is no insurance to cover the fire losses. But I think I'll be able to earn a little more money by helping Uncle Ben—at least until school starts."

Lynwood went with Sarah Beth to the chicken coop. As she let the chickens out and scattered grain for them, she said, "Which chickens do you want? We can put rings on their legs so we'll know which ones are yours. Two of the white ones are God's. You can have half of the others."

She explained that although only nineteen chickens were left, she had decided that a tithe would still be two chickens.

"It'll be several weeks before the chickens are ready to sell," Lynwood said. "Who knows what might happen before then? Maybe you should just wait until you sell your chickens. Then you'll know how much money you have, and you can easily figure out how much to tithe," he suggested. "It's not your fault that I lost the rabbits," Lynwood continued. "I won't expect you to share your profits with me."

"But I want to share," Sarah Beth insisted. "And maybe you're right about waiting until I sell the chickens to divide up the money," she admitted. "It sure would be a lot easier." She was remembering the piece of paper with all the changes and the still unknown facts.

One evening, not long after the fire, Mama and Daddy came home from a deacons' meeting at church and reported on plans to help Norma and Helen Gibson's family.

The women at church planned to collect clothing that their own children had outgrown. They would share some feed sacks, too, so that Mrs. Gibson could make clothing for the children. Church members also planned to donate surplus produce from their gardens so that the Gibsons could can food for the winter.

Some of the other churches in the city were helping, too. One businessman had offered the family a house rent-free in return for some repairs and maintenance work that Mr. Gibson could do.

Daddy said that another small factory had closed in the city. There were so many people out of work that the churches could not care for all of them. The government was helping, too. In fact, one night the family heard President Roosevelt talking on the radio. He told about thousands of men who were being put to work building roads, bridges, public buildings, and dams that the country needed. When the president had finished speaking, Daddy said that one of the roads to be built would run along the top of the Blue Ridge Mountains in Virginia. Part of that road would be only a few miles from their home.

Everyone was enjoying the new radio. Sarah Beth and Lynwood especially liked the thrilling drama series about Daniel Boone. It was broadcast five days a week. While listening to one of the programs, Sarah Beth got so excited that she yelled, "Look out!" when a bear was about to attack Daniel Boone.

"I don't think he can hear you," Lynwood laughed.

And to everyone's surprise, Grandma began to listen to some of the preachers on the radio.

"Do the preachers belong to our church?" Lynwood asked his grandma on one occasion.

"No," Grandma admitted. "But they all say some good things," she allowed, "even if they don't believe just the same as we do."

It was Saturday afternoon and Lynwood and Sarah Beth went to town with Mama and Daddy. Both of the children had outgrown their well-worn shoes. Several shoe stores were having sales, and Mama figured shoes would be cheaper now than they would be in September.

Lynwood went with Daddy to shop for shoes, and Sarah Beth went with Mama. Sarah Beth tried on several pairs of shoes. She looked longingly at a pair of shiny black slippers with a pretty bow, but she didn't ask to try them on. One of the girls in her Sunday school class had a pair of shoes like them. The girl wore them to church but had another pair for school. Sarah Beth knew that the shoes she bought would need to be practical ones because she would have to wear them for both church and school.

Sarah Beth and Mama finally agreed on a pair of sturdy brown oxfords. They had enough room to allow her feet to grow a little before the shoes were too tight to wear. And if she tied the laces tight, the shoes wouldn't slip up and down now.

Sarah Beth and Mama went to Woolworth's next. Mama bought a pair of stockings, some hairpins, and paraffin to seal glass jars of jelly and jam. Next they went to People's Drug Store to get some hay fever medicine for Grandma.

When the two had finished shopping, Mama and Sarah Beth went to Pugh's Department Store to meet Daddy and Lynwood. The family always met at the Salem Avenue exit of Pugh's after shopping, because it was near the lot where they parked.

Lynwood and Daddy were not there yet. "I imagine Daddy and Lynwood went down to the farmers' market," Sarah Beth said. "I wonder if they'll notice what price chickens are bringing now." Then she added, "I know it's too soon to be thinking about that. I mustn't count my chickens before they are sold."

Near the area where Sarah Beth and Mama waited, there were bolts of fabrics stacked on tables. Mama admired the beautiful materials.

"May I help you?" a clerk asked.

"Not right now, thank you," Mama answered. "I'm just looking."

Sarah Beth noticed that Mama lingered over a rich brown fabric with ivory swirls. "That's beautiful," Sarah Beth said. "It looks like coffee with ribbons of thick cream before you stir it up."

Mama smiled at her daughter's description. "It is a lovely fabric," Mama agreed.

Sarah Beth felt the soft, silky material. "Why don't you buy it?" Sarah Beth suggested. "Don't you need a new dress for your trip to the state convention this fall?"

Sarah Beth noticed that Mama glanced slyly at the price as she laid the bolt of material back on the table. "I think my navy blue dress will be fine for the trip," Mama said. "Maybe I can put a new collar and new buttons on it."

Sarah Beth wondered if Mama wanted the pretty fabric as much as Sarah Beth wanted her to have it. It would look so beautiful with Mama's dark brown eyes and hair.

Her thoughts were interrupted by Daddy and Lynwood's arrival. Sure enough, they had been to the farmers' market. But Sarah Beth didn't think to ask about the price of chickens. Her mind was still focused on Mama's need for a new dress. When a woman became a mama, did she stop wanting things for herself? Sarah Beth would ask Grandma about that sometime.

෴

Summer was passing quickly. Old Dominicker weaned her brood of chickens. She gradually pushed them away from her, forcing them to fend for themselves. Finally, she went back to the chicken house with the other hens and left the chickens on their own.

Sarah Beth still kept a watchful eye on the chickens. When it rained, she made sure they were in the coop. She continued to feed them twice a day. She fastened the door of the coop securely each night.

One evening as she fed the chickens, Sarah Beth noticed that one of the Dominicker chickens was missing. She counted all the chickens again just to be sure. Only eighteen chickens. Yes, one was definitely missing. Sarah Beth looked in the coop and under some nearby bushes. She anxiously searched the backyard, the pasture, and everywhere within the range that the chickens usually covered during the day. There was not one sign of the missing chicken anywhere.

When Sarah Beth told Lynwood about the missing chicken, he said, "A hawk probably got it. Uncle Ben mentioned that he saw a chicken hawk last week."

Sarah Beth knew that one of these big birds of prey could swoop down and carry off a young chicken in its claws. She wondered if Old Dominicker could have scared the hawk away if she had still been with the brood. Would the hawk return and steal other chickens? Sarah Beth was worried. Were there other dangers she had not even thought of that might threaten the remaining chickens?

# CHAPTER 6

# A Birthday Surprise

When Sarah Beth opened her eyes, the sun was peeping through the open window. The light breeze that rippled the curtains was already warm. She wondered if it was hot and sunny on this day ten years ago—the day that she was born.

Once she had seen Daddy's pocket diary for that year. The only entry for August 5 was "A baby girl born this morning!" She wondered what thoughts were going through Daddy's mind when he ended that entry with an exclamation point.

Sarah Beth knew there would be a birthday cake with candles, her favorite foods, and perhaps a small gift by her plate at suppertime. But before that, there was work to do.

Uncle Ben had told Sarah Beth and Lynwood that he would pay them ten cents for each bushel of beans they picked. After Sarah Beth finished breakfast and fed her chickens, she went with her brother to Uncle Ben's bean patch. Uncle Ben set an empty bushel basket at the end of a row and handed Sarah Beth a bucket. "When your basket is full, I'll get you another one," he said.

Lynwood was picking in the next row. Two of her older cousins were also picking. The green beans hung thick on the lush vines. Sarah Beth began to pull the beans quickly and dropped them into the bucket. Even so, everyone else was soon ahead of her.

At last her bucket was filled. When she emptied it into the basket at the end of her row, the bottom of the basket was barely covered. Lynwood had said it would take eight buckets to fill the basket.

Before her bucket was filled again, her arms and legs itched where the vines rubbed them. Sweat ran from under her sunbonnet down over her forehead. The row of bean vines seemed to stretch endlessly before her.

How many beans will it take to make a bushel? she wondered. Only the thought of a shiny dime to add to her savings jar kept her going.

Before the basket at the end of Sarah Beth's row was filled, the vines had been stripped of beans in all the rows except the one where she was picking. Her cousin Jennie came over with a bucket partly filled with beans. "My basket wouldn't hold these," she said as she poured them into Sarah Beth's basket. Jennie helped Sarah Beth finish her row. When the two girls emptied their buckets into Sarah Beth's basket, it was heaped up and running over.

Uncle Ben dropped two dimes into Sarah Beth's hand. "One for your good work," he said, "and one for your birthday."

If I live to be a hundred years old, I'll never get rich picking beans, Sarah Beth thought as she wiped the sweat from her face.

After dinner, when Sarah Beth started to clear the dishes from the table, Mama said, "No more chores for you today. It's your birthday. You may do whatever you wish until suppertime."

Sarah Beth went to the telephone on the wall in the front hall. She lifted the receiver from the hook on one side of the wooden box and held it to her ear. She turned the little handle on the other side of the box—one long, slow turn—a pause—a short quick turn—another pause—and then another long, slow turn. She heard one long, one short, one long ring. Mary's mama answered.

Sarah Beth stood on tiptoe to speak into the mouthpiece on the box. She politely inquired about Mrs. Adams' health and then asked if Mary could come to her house to play. "Mary is away visiting her grandma," Mrs. Adams said.

Disappointed, Sarah Beth thanked Mrs. Adams and hung up the telephone receiver. Then she got her favorite doll and went down the hill to the spring. She climbed up on the rock wall that separated the spring and springhouse from the pasture. The broad leaves of a huge sycamore tree shaded her from the sun. A breeze blowing across the icy spring water cooled her skin.

Sarah Beth loved this spot. Sometimes she and Lynwood fished for crawdads in the spring branch. Sometimes they put homemade paddle boats into the water or floated small cucumbers with sails on toothpicks until the cucumbers were chilled and crisp enough to eat. Once they had built a dam across a narrow part of the branch.

Today Sarah Beth just sat quietly. She looked across the pasture where the cows, Blossom and Josephine, and Old Dolly, the horse, grazed in the shade of a tree. Beyond the pasture fence, a neighbor's field of late oats rippled in the breeze just like the song they sang at school—"amber waves of grain."

There were mountains in the distance. It was obvious why these mountains were called the Blue Ridge. Today the breeze sent clouds scudding across the sun's face and made shadows playfully race up the mountainside, mixing deep purple with the shades of blue.

Sarah Beth examined the clouds. They weren't storm clouds. No need to worry about her chickens. She listened to the soft murmur of the water as it flowed over stones. The distant sound of a train whistle caught her attention.

"I wonder where that train goes," Sarah Beth said to her doll, Samantha. "Daddy says it goes over the mountain. Someday I'll ride a train over that mountain and see what is on the other side."

Sarah Beth remembered one fine Sunday afternoon when Daddy had taken the family for a drive up Catawba Mountain. Winding around the hairpin-shaped curves had made Sarah Beth's stomach churn. When they reached the top of the mountain, the other side looked the same as their side. There was a valley with farms and houses and then another mountain.

A crackling KAK-KAK-KAK shattered the peaceful stillness and Sarah Beth's reverie. Anxiously she searched the skies and located the menacing chicken hawk. It was flying away from the farm with a small wild rabbit in its claws. The chickens were safe—for now. Was that hawk responsible for the disappearance of one of her chickens last week? Sarah Beth shook her fist at the vanishing bird.

"Grandma was right," Sarah Beth confided to Samantha. "I counted my chickens way too soon. No matter how careful I am, bad things happen that I can't control. I know now that I'll have nowhere near enough money for the fancy dollhouse in the magazine ad—or the furniture and tiny doll family."

"Besides," she added, "I'm getting pretty fond of those chickens. I couldn't ever help dress them for market." Sarah Beth remembered with distaste the process of plucking the feathers from chickens and cleaning out their insides. "Maybe I'll just sell my chickens alive even though they'll bring a lot less money that way."

"It'll be best to wait until the chickens are sold before deciding how to spend the money," Sarah Beth told Samantha. "One shouldn't count her chickens before they are hatched—and sold. After I divide the money with Lynwood, I might have enough for a small dollhouse without furniture and dolls."

☙

On the supper table beside Sarah Beth's plate lay a package—a Big Little Book, she guessed. These popular books, thick and four-inch square, were hard to disguise in a package. Also, in the corner of the room was a big box with a pink bow painted on top. Sarah Beth could not imagine what was in that box.

When everyone was ready for dessert, Mama brought in a chocolate cake with ten twinkling candles on it. Sarah Beth made a wish and blew out every candle. Then she opened the package by her plate—a Big Little Book that she had been wanting. On the cover was a picture of Shirley Temple, a very young movie star.

While Sarah Beth was thumbing through the book, Daddy called attention to the box in the corner of the room. "Now open the big box," he said to his daughter.

Her eyes wide with excitement, Sarah Beth tore open the box. First she pulled out five empty boxes, each open on one side. With the boxes was a birthday note from Daddy.

Along with a note from Mama were scraps of fabric and lace and pieces of wallpaper.

From Lynwood there was a stack of cardboard backs from school tablets, small empty matchboxes, and a bag of spools.

Inside an envelope from Grandma was a card on which was printed

GIFT CERTIFICATE
FOR
POTS OF PASTE
AS NEEDED
FOR CONSTRUCTION PROJECT

There was also a big bag filled with tiny scraps of paper along with a card with a few scribbled pencil marks on it, under which Mama had written Will's name.

At the very bottom of the box was a watercolor painting by Lynwood. The dollhouse in the painting was labeled TENTATIVE DESIGN FOR SARAH BETH MILLER'S DOLL MANSION.

Sarah Beth was overwhelmed by her family's wonderful gift. In her imagination she could see how the boxes could form a house. She pictured papered walls and curtained windows. A spool topped with a circle of cardboard and lace would make a fine table. A small matchbox on half of a spool split lengthwise would be a perfect baby cradle, and... Her mind was filled with ways to create all kinds of furniture.

She smiled as her eyes rested on the huge bag of tiny paper scraps. They were useless, of course, but it was sweet of Will to want to share with her the bits of paper that he so loved to tear up. After Mama put Will to bed that night, Sarah Beth picked up the bag of paper scraps and started to take them to the trash box in the kitchen.

"Wait," said Lynwood, "we'll need all those scraps and more."

"Whatever for?" she asked.

"You'll see," Lynwood smiled mysteriously.

In bed that night, Sarah Beth lay awake for a long time. Her head was filled with visions of a fine dollhouse and all kinds of furniture. And her heart was filled with gratitude for a wonderful family who loved her and wanted to make her dream come true.

∞

When Sarah Beth woke up the next morning, she wanted to start work on her dollhouse immediately. But Daddy announced at breakfast that tomatoes were ready for canning. He had picked half a bushel and brought them to the house. There were lots more ripe ones in the garden waiting to be harvested.

After Daddy had gone to work, Mama, Lynwood, and Sarah Beth went to the garden to finish picking tomatoes. Grandma put several pots of water on the stove to boil. Then she brought boxes of tin cans and lids from the basement and washed them.

When all the tomatoes had been picked and brought to the house, Grandma poured boiling water over them. Then she and Lynwood slipped the hot skins from the tomatoes. Mama and Sarah Beth packed the peeled tomatoes into the tin cans. As the cans were filled, a lid was placed on each one. One by one the cans were set on the capping machine, and a few turns of a handle sealed the lid.

The sealed cans were carried to the washhouse where water was boiling in a big iron kettle over a wood fire that Grandma had started earlier. The cans were placed in the water and boiled for thirty minutes. Finally they were moved to a table where they would stay until they cooled down.

The tomato canning project plus all the regular chores made a full day. Everyone was tired. Still, after supper, Sarah Beth got out the construction materials for her dollhouse. She arranged and rearranged the five boxes until she found an arrangement that pleased her—three rooms downstairs and two upstairs. She wasn't surprised to find that it was almost exactly like Lynwood's drawing.

The Millers' home had eight rooms—four bedrooms upstairs and a kitchen, a dining room, a sitting room, and a parlor downstairs.

The dollhouse in the magazine ad had seven rooms. Sarah Beth had a hard time deciding what the five rooms in her dollhouse would be. Obviously, the two rooms upstairs would be bedrooms. One room downstairs would be the kitchen. It was a large room. It could also be the dining room, Sarah Beth decided. What about the other two rooms? A parlor and a sitting room? Or a sitting room and a bedroom?

We don't use our parlor very much, Sarah Beth thought. Just when we have company or want to sing around the piano. In the winter we keep the parlor door closed most of the time so we don't have to heat that room. Maybe my dollhouse doesn't need a parlor, but it could have a fine rug and a piano in the sitting room.

Sarah Beth thought about the doll family she hoped to get for the house. There would be a mother and father, some girls and some boys, maybe a grandmother. Three bedrooms would definitely be needed. It was all settled. Two bedrooms upstairs. A bedroom, a kitchen-dining room, and a parlor-sitting room downstairs. First thing tomorrow she would put the rooms together with paste and begin to decorate them.

When tomorrow came, the house construction had to be postponed once more. The corn in the garden was ready to be canned. Everyone was needed to help. Canning corn was even more work that canning tomatoes. After the ears of corn were shucked, each one had to be scrubbed with a brush to remove the silky fibers that grew between the rows of corn. Then the grains of corn had to be cut from the cob and packed into the cans.

When the cans of corn were finally boiling in the big iron kettle, Sarah Beth went to her room and arranged the boxes for her dollhouse. With a pencil, she made small Xs where she thought the windows and doors should be. Lynwood's sketch made it easy to decide where the windows and outside door would be. It took longer to decide where to place the doors between the rooms. She had to think about the location of the stairs and the placement of the furniture.

Finally she was satisfied with her decisions about the position of all the doors and windows. Using a ruler, she started outlining the openings to be cut in the walls. Getting the windows straight and properly aligned with one another proved harder than she had imagined. She had to do a lot of erasing. She was still not satisfied with her work when she had to leave the dollhouse and begin her evening chores.

Sarah Beth counted her chickens as she fed them. There were still eighteen of them—eleven pullets and seven roosters. They were almost big enough to sell. Sarah Beth would soon have her dollhouse, and she had lots of ideas for making furniture. She would have to rethink her plans for spending the money she would earn. Perhaps she would still buy some small dolls.

There was no more time to work on the dollhouse that day. After a very light supper, the family went to an ice cream social at the Independent Church near the foot of the mountain. Almost everyone in the community was there—Baptists, Methodists, Brethren, Lutherans, even an Episcopalian family from town, plus quite a few others who never darkened any church door except for weddings and funerals. Neighbors, divided by different beliefs on Sundays, were united at an ice cream social by food and fellowship, no matter which church sponsored it.

There were freezers full of homemade ice cream of many flavors and every kind of pie, cobbler, cake, and cookie that one could imagine. There were games and contests and singing and lots of old-fashioned visiting. Men compared farm prices, wondered how long the drought would continue, and discussed President Roosevelt's latest efforts to halt the depression.

Women shared recipes for using the bumper crop of summer squash, traded printed feed sacks, inquired about the sick, and discussed which women were having babies. Children enjoyed comparing summer activities with classmates they had not seen since school closed in the spring.

Late that night when the Millers were on their way home, Grandma called attention to the crescent moon. "See how the moon is tipped forward," she explained to Sarah Beth and Lynwood. "That means rain will be poured out. It's a sure sign of coming rain. The Farmer's Almanac also calls for rain tomorrow," she added.

Sarah Beth and Lynwood looked toward Daddy, but it was too dark in the car to see his face. They knew that Daddy did not always share Grandma's reliance on the Almanac, but tonight Daddy was silent. He just hoped Grandma was right. Rain would surely be welcome.

# CHAPTER 7

# Building Is Better Than Buying

Before Sarah Beth opened her eyes, she heard a refreshing sound—raindrops on the metal porch roof outside her bedroom window. Usually this sound would cause her to lie still and enjoy the thought of thirsty crops drinking up rain. Today she sat up quickly. Because it was raining, there would be more time to work on the dollhouse.

Sarah Beth looked across the room toward the boxes that she had labored to mark with windows and doors. She couldn't believe her eyes. The boxes were sitting on a low, unpainted table, and the openings she had struggled to mark were cleanly cut out and perfectly aligned. Sarah Beth wondered how early Daddy must have risen to do this for her.

When Sarah Beth reached the kitchen, Lynwood was already up. He was emptying Will's bits of scrap paper into a large mixing bowl. "What on earth are you doing?" Sarah Beth wanted to know.

"You'll see—just be patient," he teased with a mysterious grin. He drew water into a pan and poured it over the paper. "The paper will have to soak in the water for several hours," he explained.

As soon as the breakfast dishes were washed, Grandma started a pot of paste for the construction project. She knew how to make paste for any purpose by mixing together flour, water, a little salt, some alum, sometimes a little sugar. Then she boiled these ingredients to just the right consistency. This first batch of paste was needed for heavy-duty construction.

When the paste had been boiled to perfection and cooled, Sarah Beth and Lynwood pasted the five boxes together. Then they fashioned a slanting roof from two sides of a large cardboard box. They considered making roof tiles from construction paper, but Sarah Beth decided that would take too long. She was eager to complete the house. Mama said they could use leftover paint if they could find what they wanted in the basement.

Sarah Beth couldn't decide between a green roof and a gray roof. Lynwood said the green paint they found looked pretty bright for a roof, so she chose the slate gray paint. The children took turns painting the roof. Sarah Beth knew her brother was a much better painter than she, so she asked him to use a fine brush to outline shingles on the roof. In the meantime, she made a cardboard chimney, covered it with red construction paper, and drew bricks on it with a crayon.

Sarah Beth wanted to paint the outside of the house next, but Lynwood persuaded her to wait until afternoon. So, while the paste and paint were drying, Sarah Beth got out the wallpaper samples. There were so many pretty colors and patterns that it was hard to choose. She decided on a seafoam green with delicate pink flowers for one upstairs bedroom. For the other upstairs bedroom, she chose a white lacy pattern on a very pale pink background. For the bedroom downstairs, Sarah Beth chose paper with a lavender background. For the living room-parlor, she selected an ivory paper with a faint hint of a swirl pattern, and for the kitchen-dining room she selected a solid green paper. Then she found a border with a strawberry pattern to brighten the cooking area of the room.

Sarah Beth decided that before she started to paper the walls, she should finish the windows that Daddy had cut out. "I wish I had some isinglass for the window panes. Do you know where we could find some?" Sarah Beth asked Lynwood.

Lynwood could think of no place to find isinglass, so the children decided to ask Mama what else might be used for windows. "I think waxed paper might work," she suggested. "Pioneers sometimes used oiled paper over window openings."

Waxed paper with construction paper for frames will make quite acceptable windows, Sarah Beth thought. She and Lynwood spent the rest of the morning and part of the afternoon making and inserting the windows.

Finally Lynwood said, "Let's get the outside of the house ready to paint."

"What do you mean, get it ready to paint?" Sarah Beth wanted to know.

"You'll see," he said. There was that mysterious smile again. "It's time to use Will's contribution to your house."

While Grandma used a recipe that Lynwood gave her to make another pot of paste, Lynwood drained the water from the bowl in which the scraps of paper had been soaking. He asked Sarah Beth to help him squeeze the water from the scraps. They even let Will help.

Next Lynwood dumped the mushy paper scraps into the paste, and Grandma stirred them vigorously. When Grandma pronounced the mixture cool enough to handle, Lynwood took a handful and began to smear it over one side of the dollhouse.

Before Sarah Beth could protest that he was ruining her house, Lynwood exclaimed, "Voila! Stucco! When it's dry and painted, it will look just like that fine big house we saw in South Roanoke."

Lynwood was right. Sarah Beth, Mama, and Grandma all agreed. "Look," Mama explained to Will, "the little bits of paper you tore up will help make your sister's dollhouse very pretty." Will smiled happily. Although he did not completely understand what all the excitement was about, he felt a part of it.

"This is fun," Sarah Beth said as she applied a handful of glob and used her fingers to create a design in it. While she and Lynwood covered the sides of the house with stucco, Lynwood explained that the mixture was called papier-mâché. He had read about using it to make paperweights and other objects, so he figured it ought to work as stucco on the house too. Soon the outside of the house was covered. Until it dried, nothing more could be done. Sarah Beth could hardly wait for Daddy to see how Lynwood's marvelous idea had turned out.

As soon as Daddy got home, she showed him the dollhouse and thanked him for cutting out the doors and windows and for making the table on which the house now sat. Daddy agreed that it was indeed a marvelous house.

When the stucco on the dollhouse had thoroughly dried, Sarah Beth asked Lynwood to paint the house. She knew that he would enjoy this job. They found some leftover white paint in the basement. There was also the green paint they had found earlier.

"Would you like for me to paint a yard on the table top around the house?" Lynwood asked.

Sarah Beth thought that was a splendid idea. When Lynwood had finished painting the house white, he painted an expansive green yard around it. At last, both children stood back and admired the magnificent house.

In the days that followed, Sarah Beth worked on the house whenever she had a few moments to herself. She papered the walls, and Mama helped her make curtains for the windows: lacy curtains for the parlor, ruffled ones of solid-colored fabrics for the bedrooms, print ones with tiebacks for the kitchen. One day while they were working together, Sarah Beth said to Mama, "Who would have thought that making a dollhouse could be so much more fun than buying one?"

Sarah Beth constructed some stairs from cardboard but was dismayed at how much space they took up in the room. Once again Lynwood came to the rescue with a suggestion that stairs could be painted on the wall. And once again Sarah Beth asked him to do the painting. When he had finished, the stairs looked just like real ones.

"Could you paint a fireplace in the living room-parlor?" Sarah Beth asked her brother.

"Sure," he replied.

Before long, there was a fireplace in the room. Now it was time to add furniture. Day by day Sarah Beth made furniture using the spools and cardboard she had received. Grandma helped her make tiny pillows for the beds and cushions for the sofa and parlor chairs. Grandma also showed Sarah Beth how to make a braided rug for the floor in the parlor.

Sometimes Sarah Beth turned to the dollhouse and furniture in the magazine ad for ideas of things she could make, but not once did she think about buying furniture. It was so much more fun to make it. She still thought she might possibly buy some dolls when she sold her chickens. There were also a couple of other ideas in the back of her mind for using that money. For one thing, she still wanted to give Lynwood some money to help him buy a bicycle. She hadn't asked him recently how much he still needed.

Sarah Beth still had eighteen chickens, but she had long since stopped trying to figure out exactly how much money she would get for them. It wouldn't be too long now until they were ready to sell. When the money was actually in her savings jar, she could decide how to spend it.

∞

Thanks to the water from the spring used for irrigation, the Millers' garden was producing more tomatoes and squash than the family could use. "I don't think I can possibly can more vegetables right now," Mama said one evening. "I think we have enough canned tomatoes and squash to last for a couple of years."

Daddy said that he would take some of the surplus vegetables to the Gibson family. Later that evening, he came back from the Gibsons with a bicycle—or, more accurately, the remains of a bicycle, Sarah Beth thought as she looked at the two flat tires and dust-caked frame. Why did Daddy bring that crummy piece of junk home with him? she wondered. But before she blurted out the question, she caught a glimpse of Lynwood's face. He actually seemed pleased. Sarah Beth couldn't imagine how that could be possible, but she kept her mouth shut.

"Mr. Gibson found this bike in a garage he cleaned out for the man who owns the house where the Gibsons live," Daddy explained. "The man told him to get rid of the bike."

"This was a very expensive bike," Lynwood said as he ran his hand over the dusty frame. "It's a real top-of-the-line Schwinn."

"It was evidently stored for a long time," Daddy said. "Dry rot has ruined the tires, but the rest of the bike is in good condition."

Lynwood was excited. "With new tires and a coat of paint, the bike will be as good as new," he exclaimed.

Sarah Beth was deep in thought. I saw only a dirty, discarded piece of junk, but Lynwood can visualize a shiny new bicycle. Is that because he knows more about bikes than I do, she wondered, or is there just a difference between Lynwood and me? She suspected the latter was true. Or could it be that seeing possibilities is learned by practice?

Sarah Beth was remembering the dollhouse. It would never have occurred to her to make her own house. But now she thought of new ways to make furniture and new things to add to the house almost every day. Then her thoughts returned to the bike. She was happy for her brother. "It won't be long until I sell my chickens," she said to him. "I can help you pay for new tires and paint."

"Thanks," Lynwood said, "but I think with the money I have saved and with what I've earned helping Uncle Ben this summer, I'll have enough to restore the bike to first-rate condition."

Sarah Beth listened as Lynwood and Daddy continued to talk. She closed her eyes and tried to picture in her mind the bicycle as her brother must see it. She saw a possibility that neither Lynwood nor Daddy had discussed. She decided not to mention her idea right now. A secret plan was forming in her mind.

꩜

A few days later the phone rang. After talking for a few minutes, Mama said, "Sarah Beth, Uncle Ben wants to speak to you."

Sarah Beth was surprised. Uncle Ben said, "Today on the market, a lady asked if I knew where she could buy some young pullets. She wants to add young hens to her flock of egg layers. Are those chickens of yours ready to sell?"

"I think so," Sarah Beth answered.

"How many pullets do you have?"

"Eleven." Sarah Beth replied. "Three Dominickers, three white Leghorns, and five Rhode Island Reds."

"And how old are they?" her uncle asked.

"They hatched the day after school was out last spring," she responded. She paused to think for a minute. "That would make them almost twelve weeks old," she added.

Uncle Ben promised to ask the lady if she would like to buy the eleven pullets. But he told Sarah Beth he was not sure the woman would want a flock of mixed breeds. Sarah Beth was very excited about the possibility of selling the pullets as layers and told the family about her conversation with Uncle Ben.

"Will you dress the roosters and sell them as fryers?" Lynwood wanted to know. "That's the way to get the most money for them."

"I know," Sarah Beth said slowly. "But I could never help pluck their feathers or dress them. I've cared for them too long and know them too well. Maybe Uncle Ben can take them to market and sell them alive. I'll ask him."

That evening when Sarah Beth fed her chickens, she counted them as she always did. Only this time she looked at each one with fondness. She would be glad to sell them and have the money for which she had worked all summer. Still she would miss her chickens.

The next afternoon Sarah Beth asked if she could walk over to Uncle Ben's. She was eager to know if the lady wanted her pullets.

"You could just call him," Mama suggested.

"I know," Sarah Beth said, "but it would be nice to visit with Aunt Emma, too. I haven't been to their house for a long time."

Mama agreed, and Sarah Beth walked over to her aunt and uncle's home. Uncle Ben said that the lady who had talked to him about pullets would probably buy all of Sarah Beth's future layers. She would discuss price when she saw the pullets.

"That's great," Sarah Beth said. "Do you think you could also sell the seven roosters live on the market?" she asked.

Her uncle felt sure that he could sell them individually. He suggested that he take the pullets and roosters to market the following Saturday. "Could I go with you when you take my chickens?" Sarah Beth asked. "I'd like to shop for a couple of things as soon as I have some money from the sale."

"Your uncle won't have time to shop with you, and your mama wouldn't want you to shop alone," Aunt Emma interrupted before Uncle Ben could answer. "But I've been wanting to do some shopping myself," she continued. "Maybe we could shop together."

Sarah Beth thought that was a splendid idea. She could use Aunt Emma's help in shopping for one of the items on her list. "There are two things I want to buy," Sarah Beth told her aunt, "but I don't want my family to know." She told Aunt Emma all about a plan that had been forming in her mind.

Aunt Emma was pleased with her niece's plan and promised to help her without giving away Sarah Beth's secret.

When Sarah Beth started to leave, Aunt Emma called to her, "Wait a minute. I have something I've been meaning to give you." She handed her niece several pages torn from magazines. On each page were a paper doll and some clothes to cut out.

"Oh, thank you," Sarah Beth said excitedly. "These will be perfect to play with in my dollhouse."

"Each month I get a magazine that has a paper doll with clothes. I'll save them for you as I finish reading the magazines," her aunt promised.

Sarah Beth practically flew home. She had so much to share with Mama and the rest of the family. As soon as she entered the door, she spilled out the details of the plans to sell her chickens. Mama agreed that Sarah Beth could go with her uncle and aunt when they took the chickens to market.

Assuming that he would go along, Lynwood said, "It'll be fun having you with us on market day."

But Mama had a different idea. "You often go with Uncle Ben to market," she said to Lynwood. "I think this should be a special day just for Sarah Beth. Besides, there probably isn't room in the truck for both of you along with Uncle Ben and Aunt Emma.

# CHAPTER 8

# Market Day

Sarah Beth could hardly wait for Saturday to come. Every night she counted her chickens to be sure they were all still there and well.

On Friday Aunt Emma called to say that Uncle Ben would pick up Sarah Beth and her chickens at 5 o'clock on Saturday morning. Aunt Emma would ride to town with a neighbor and join them on the market later in the day. Five o'clock was much earlier than Sarah Beth usually got up. "No matter," she told her mama. "I probably won't sleep a wink all night. I'm too excited."

After supper that night, Daddy went to the barn and got two flat cages used for transporting chickens. He helped Sarah Beth put the pullets in one cage and the roosters in the other. They set the cages inside the chicken house and carefully closed the door.

When she finally fell asleep that night, Sarah Beth dreamed about saying goodbye to the chickens she had cared for during so many weeks. She awoke early and was ready to go when her uncle arrived to load the chickens. Uncle Ben had already packed his truck bed with fresh vegetables to sell that day, leaving just enough room for the two chicken coops. Sarah Beth climbed into the cab of the truck beside her uncle.

When they reached the city market and pulled into Uncle Ben's regular stall, the market was bustling. Many farmers were arriving and setting out the produce they hoped to sell that day. Uncle Ben set the chicken cages on the shady side of the truck. Then he arranged the vegetables and put prices on them. A few farmers displayed their produce on tables, but Uncle Ben, like most of the sellers, sold from the back of his truck. Today Uncle Ben had bushels of tomatoes, corn, summer squash, eggplants, green peppers, butter beans, several kinds of greens, grapes, and eggs.

Customers were beginning to arrive. These early buyers were storekeepers who bought large quantities of vegetables that they would resell in their stores. When this first wave of selling was over and things had slowed down, Uncle Ben said to Sarah Beth, "I want to see who else has chickens to sell today and what they're charging for them. I won't be gone long. You can sell to any customers who come by."

Uncle Ben showed his niece the box where he kept change and put money from the sales. Then he was off. Sarah Beth felt very important. She had listened to Lynwood talk about selling on the market. Now it was her turn. While her uncle was gone, she sold several tomatoes, four peppers, and a few ears of corn. She carefully counted out change, politely thanked each customer, and placed the money in the box.

When Uncle Ben returned, he said, "You're lucky today. There aren't many fryers on the market. So they are bringing a good price—about 22 cents a pound."

"I hope lots of people are hungry for fried chicken so I can sell all my roosters," Sarah Beth said.

Before long a woman stopped to inquire about fryers. She wanted chickens to fry for a family reunion. She looked at the roosters in the coop and pointed to two. "Please weigh those two and tell me how much they will cost," she said.

Uncle Ben took the roosters out one by one, tied their feet together with binder twine, and weighed them. "Together they weigh just over six pounds," he told the lady. "At 22 cents a pound that will come to $1.32.

"That will be just fine," the lady said as she reached into her pocketbook for money.

"You can pay the young lady here." Uncle Ben nodded toward Sarah Beth. "She raised these chickens."

Sarah Beth beamed as the lady handed her $1.40 and told her to keep the change. She thanked the lady profusely. When Uncle Ben handed the frightened, struggling roosters to the customer, Sarah Beth turned her head away, but she couldn't shut out the loud squawks of the roosters. Maybe it would have been better if I had not insisted on helping Uncle Ben sell the chickens, she thought. On the other hand, she was somewhat consoled by the feel of the money in her hands and knowing that this was why she had cared for the chickens all summer.

It was about midmorning when Uncle Ben said to Sarah Beth, "Here comes Mrs. Saunders. She's the lady who wants to buy pullets. That must be her husband with her."

When the couple reached the truck, Mrs. Saunders greeted Uncle Ben and introduced her husband. Then, turning to Sarah Beth, she continued. "You must be the young lady who raised the chickens. Your uncle has told me about you."

"Yes, this is my niece, Sarah Beth Miller," Uncle Ben said, introducing her to Mr. and Mrs. Saunders.

Uncle Ben pulled the cage containing the pullets to the edge of the sidewalk.

"My goodness, these are very healthy looking pullets. How old did you say they are?" Mrs. Saunders asked.

"They're twelve weeks old. They hatched the day after school was out last spring," Sarah Beth explained.

"You must have taken very good care of them and fed them well," Mrs. Saunders said.

"I tried to take good care of them, but I lost two chickens during the summer. A chicken hawk got one, and one drowned during a storm." Sarah Beth was in the middle of the story about the storm when Uncle Ben suggested that Mrs. Saunders probably didn't have time to hear about all the adventures of the chickens.

Mrs. Saunders decided to buy all the pullets. "By next spring they should make good layers," she said.

Then Mrs. Saunders noticed the roosters in the other cage. "Maybe I should add a young rooster to my flock, too," she suggested. Uncle Ben slid the cage of roosters out into the sunlight. "I think I'll take that red rooster," Mrs. Saunders said, pointing to the biggest rooster in the cage.

"I've done some checking into prices for layers," Mrs. Saunders continued. "Since these are such healthy pullets and have obviously had such good care, I think we could pay 70 cents each for the pullets and the same for the rooster." Mr. Saunders agreed with his wife. "Would that be satisfactory with you?" she asked, looking at Sarah Beth.

Sarah Beth glanced at her uncle, and he nodded. "That will be quite satisfactory," she said to the buyer.

While her husband went to his truck to get a cage to transfer the chickens, Mrs. Saunders took out her purse. She counted out $8.40 and handed the money to Sarah Beth.

"Thank you very much," Sarah Beth said politely. "I hope the pullets will turn out to be fine layers for you. I'm so glad they've found a good home instead of ending up on somebody's dinner table."

When Mr. Saunders returned with a cage, Sarah Beth helped transfer the pullets and red rooster while Uncle Ben waited on another customer.

As Sarah Beth watched the Saunders walk away with her chickens, she was jubilant. She counted the money she had received for the pullets and red rooster and added it to the money received earlier for the two fryers. She had $9.80. That was better than she had dared hope for. Now only four roosters remained to be sold as fryers.

As Sarah Beth was putting her purse in Uncle Ben's money box, Aunt Emma walked up. Excitedly, Sarah Beth told her aunt all about the sale of the chickens and the sum of money she had safely tucked away. "Maybe Uncle Ben can sell the other four fryers while you and I are shopping," she suggested to her aunt. Sarah Beth would just as soon not watch the remaining roosters being tied up and taken away squawking.

"You two ladies go on shopping," Uncle Ben agreed. "I'll see if I can sell the rest of the roosters."

Sarah Beth took her money from the box. She decided to let her aunt keep it for her until she was ready to spend it. Aunt Emma suggested that since Sarah Beth had had such an early breakfast, they might like to eat lunch before shopping.

"Where are we going to eat?" Sarah Beth asked. She hoped maybe they would eat at Roanoke Wiener Stand. Lynwood had told her about buying a hot dog and Grape Nehi there when he helped Uncle Ben on the market.

But Aunt Emma had a different suggestion. "I thought we might eat at Woolworth's lunch counter," she said. Sarah Beth was a bit disappointed, but she agreed politely because she really was grateful for her aunt's help in shopping.

At the lunch counter, Aunt Emma ordered a plate lunch and iced tea. Sarah Beth decided to have a hot dog and chocolate milk. She was tempted to order a chocolate milk shake but changed her mind when she noticed the price. As they were finishing their meal, Aunt Emma suggested, "Why don't we splurge and divide a banana split for dessert? You're my guest for lunch, and this is a special day for you. You have worked hard all summer for this day," her aunt continued.

"Thank you, that would be splendid," Sarah Beth responded politely in her most ladylike tone of voice. She enjoyed the way Aunt Emma treated her—almost like a grown-up friend.

Ordinarily Sarah Beth would have eaten such a scrumptious dessert slowly, savoring each delicious bite, but today she had to force herself not to eat fast. She was so eager to begin shopping.

"Can we go to Pugh's first?" Sarah Beth asked as her aunt paid for their lunches.

"We'll go there next," her aunt agreed, "but first I want to look at a few things here."

Aunt Emma bought a couple of items, but mostly she just looked. This delight in "just looking" was something that Sarah Beth had never understood about women. Sarah Beth liked to go directly to what she wanted to buy and then move on quickly to the next item on her shopping list.

When they reached Pugh's, Sarah Beth rushed to the back of the store, directly to a stack of fine fabrics. Her eyes searched quickly through the stack. It was not there! Her heart sank. The beautiful material that her mother had admired earlier in the summer was gone.

"May I help you?" a clerk asked.

Almost frantically, Sarah Beth described the rich brown fabric with creamy swirls her mother had looked at last month. "Oh, I know exactly which fabric you mean. I remember you and your mother talking about it," the clerk smiled. "I think we still have a piece on the remnant table."

She led the way to a table stacked with premeasured goods. Sarah Beth pawed through the fabrics anxiously. Finally she found what she was looking for. She ran her hand over the fabric. It was just as soft and beautiful as she remembered.

"Do you think there is enough to make Mama a dress?" she anxiously asked her aunt. Sarah Beth had told Aunt Emma all about the fabric and her mama's need for a new dress for the meeting in Blacksburg.

Aunt Emma looked at the tag on the remnant. She assured her niece that this would be ample fabric for any pattern her mama might choose for a dress. The clerk agreed, and Sarah Beth sighed with relief. She was even more delighted when she discovered that the price of fabrics was always reduced when they were placed on the remnant table.

Aunt Emma took out her niece's purse and handed it to Sarah Beth, who counted out $2.20 and handed it to the clerk.

"That truly is a lovely piece of material," Aunt Emma said as they walked away from the fabric department. "I can just picture how beautiful your mother will look in her new dress."

Sarah Beth was walking on air. She couldn't remember when she had ever been so filled with joy.

Before they left Pugh's, Aunt Emma shopped for a gift for a new baby. She didn't find anything that satisfied her, so they crossed the street and looked at Heironimus's. Aunt Emma bought a pretty little dress that was on sale.

"Are we going to the bicycle shop next?" Sarah Beth asked her aunt.

"We'll head that way now," Aunt Emma answered. "But we'll make another stop or two along the way."

They stopped at McClellan's and then at Kress's. "I ought to get a little surprise for Will," Sarah Beth said. She bought a small package of balloons. She didn't want anyone to feel left out, so she decided on horehound candy for Grandma. Sarah Beth had tried a piece of horehound once and thought it tasted like medicine, but she knew that Grandma was very fond of it. She had a hard time thinking of a gift for Daddy. After looking at shaving lotion and handkerchiefs, she remembered seeing Daddy lace his everyday shoes with a piece of fodder twine just last week. So she bought a pair of long shoestrings for him.

The next stop was the bicycle shop. Sarah Beth had never imagined there were so many things you could add to a bicycle. After listening to Lynwood and Daddy talk about fixing up her brother's bike, she thought that a basket would be convenient for carrying things. That was something that neither Lynwood nor Daddy had mentioned. She remembered that several children carried their school books in baskets on their bikes. Maybe Lynwood would like one.

Then some horns caught her eye. The storekeeper let her sound some of the horns. There were some lights, too, but Sarah Beth didn't think her brother would ride much after dark. The storekeeper had a suggestion. "Why don't you buy a gift certificate? Then your brother can choose what he wants."

That seemed like a perfect idea to Sarah Beth. She paid the storekeeper and carefully tucked the envelope with the certificate inside into the bag with the dress fabric.

"Now I've finished my shopping," Sarah Beth announced with satisfaction.

"So have I," said Aunt Emma, after checking her list. "Let's go see if Uncle Ben has sold all his produce."

Their timing was perfect. When they reached the market, Uncle Ben was putting an empty chicken cage into the truck bed. Sarah Beth stood on tiptoe and peered into the truck. The other chicken cage was empty, too. Uncle Ben smiled at her. "Yes, I sold the rest of your roosters," he said before she could ask.

He handed Sarah Beth a little piece of paper on which he had written the weight of each fryer and the amount of money received for it. Then he counted out the money and gave it to her. Sarah Beth did a quick mental tally and estimated the total receipts for all the chickens. It was better than she had hoped. Sarah Beth carefully tucked the money and the piece of paper into her purse.

Next she took out the receipts for each of her purchases and put them into her purse. She smiled contentedly. There was some other figuring to be done, but that could wait until later.

When she got out of the truck at home, Sarah Beth gave her Uncle Ben and Aunt Emma big hugs and thanked them for their help.

As soon as Sarah Beth entered the house, Will and Lynwood wanted to see what she had bought. "You'll have to wait until later," she said. Now it was her turn to smile mysteriously.

As soon as she had taken her precious packages to her room, Sarah Beth came back downstairs and told her family all about the day, beginning with the sale of all the chickens.

That night as she set the table for supper, Sarah Beth placed a little gift at each plate. She had decided not to wrap the packages. After all it was not Christmas or someone's birthday. Besides, she hadn't thought to buy wrapping paper. So she neatly folded down the top of each bag.

When Sarah Beth stood back and looked at the table, she realized for the first time that in all of the shopping she had done that day, she hadn't bought one single thing for herself. She had not even looked at dollhouse furniture or dolls. Not at all disturbed by her realization, she was quickly reminded of the Bible verse "It is more blessed to give than to receive." She had heard the preacher repeat Acts 20:35 many times when the offering was taken at church. For the first time in her young life, Sarah Beth understood that giving really can make you happier than receiving.

When the family gathered at the supper table, Will could not wait to open the bag beside his plate. Then he wanted someone to blow up one of the balloons immediately, but Mama told him he would have to wait until after supper.

Lynwood was the next to open a bag. Sarah Beth told him excitedly about the baskets and horns and lights and all kinds of gadgets for bikes at the store. He was delighted with the prospect of shopping for himself.

Daddy and Grandma were also very pleased with their unexpected gifts. As usual, Mama had waited until last to open her gift. This time Sarah Beth was glad that Mama was last, for Mama's gift was the one that pleased Sarah Beth the most.

When Mama opened her bag and pulled out the fine fabric, her eyes filled with tears. Sarah Beth could see that behind the tears there was sheer happiness. Mama was speechless. But when she went over and hugged her daughter, Sarah Beth could feel Mama's delight and gratitude. Words would come later. At that moment, none were necessary.

# CHAPTER 9

# So Many Changes

Sarah Beth was so tired and so filled with happiness on Saturday night that she went straight to bed after family devotions. She tucked her purse into a drawer without even counting her money.

After the dinner dishes were washed on Sunday, Sarah Beth went to her room. She had some bookkeeping to do. She got out the scraps of paper with notes about the sale of her chickens and the receipts for the purchases she had made. On a piece of paper, she recorded the money she had received and the money she had spent.

| | |
|---|---|
| 11 pullets & 1 rooster | $ 8.40 |
| 2 roosters, 6 lbs. @ $.22 per lb., plus tip | $ 1.40 |
| 1 rooster, 3 1/4 lbs. @ $.22 per lb. | $ .71 |
| 1 rooster, 2 3/4 lbs. @ $ .22 per lb. | $ .60 |
| 2 roosters, 6 1/4 lbs. @ $ .22 per lb. | $ 1.37 |
| TOTAL RECEIVED | $12.48 |
| | |
| Dress fabric | $ 2.20 |
| Gift certificate | $ 1.00 |
| Candy | $ .10 |
| Shoestrings | $ .10 |
| Balloons | $ .05 |
| TOTAL SPENT | $ 3.45 |

Sarah Beth subtracted the amount spent from the amount received. I should have $ 9.03, she noted. She counted the money in her purse and smiled. She had exactly that much money. Then Sarah Beth got her savings jar and counted the coins she had either saved or earned earlier. When she added the chicken money, she had a total of $11.23.

Sarah Beth put the savings jar back in the drawer and pulled out a piece of paper. Unfolding it, she looked at the problem she had carefully stated last May.

Can I earn enough money from the sale of 24 chickens to buy a dollhouse, some furniture, and some dolls?

| | |
|---|---|
| Dollhouse | $ 8.50 |
| Furniture | $ 2.25 |
| Small dolls | $ 1.50 |
| TOTAL NEEDED | $12.25 |

3 lbs. per fryer × $_____ per lb. = $_____ per fryer

~~22~~ ~~24~~ fryers × $_____ per fryer = $_____

18 ~~20~~ ~~19~~

It seemed so long ago that she had stated that problem. And so many things had changed. She looked at the crossed out numbers. Grandma was so right. Sarah Beth remembered the fable about the milkmaid. You shouldn't count your chickens before they hatched. In fact, you really couldn't count them until they were sold.

She had expected twenty-four chickens, but the hen could cover only twenty-two eggs. Two of the eggs had not hatched. One chicken had drowned; a hawk had stolen another. Less than half of the chickens were sold as fryers; none had been plucked and dressed for sale as she had originally planned.

Sarah Beth looked at the paper again. The numbers were not the only thing that had changed during the summer. She glanced fondly at the dollhouse in her room. What pleasure she had had in making it! She no longer had any desire to buy the dollhouse in the magazine ad.

Almost every day Sarah Beth thought of a way to make some new piece of furniture for the house. If a room became too crowded, she stored some of the original pieces in a box.

And what about the dolls? Right now Sarah Beth had a whole family of paper dolls—the ones Aunt Emma had given her and some she had cut from an old catalog and pasted on construction paper. Maybe I'll still order dolls someday, Sarah Beth thought.

She still had one thing to figure out. She recalled her earlier decision that one-tenth of her chickens belonged to God. She remembered Lynwood's suggestion that it would be easier to figure one-tenth of her total earnings than to keep track of which chickens were God's. He was certainly right.

Sarah Beth looked at the figure $12.48, her earnings. She mentally moved the decimal point one place to the left. Her tithe would be $1.25. Did two white chickens bring exactly that amount? she wondered. Not that it mattered in the least, of course.

How much of the tithe money would she give at the special harvest offering in the fall? The harvest offering would help build a church or school in Nigeria. Sarah Beth remembered the missionary teacher who spoke at church last spring. The visitor had talked about boys and girls who had no church and no school and who had never heard about Jesus. Maybe she would give all the tithe money to help the children in Nigeria. She decided to give more thought to that later.

Right now she would join her family in the sitting room. Maybe Lynwood would be ready for a game of checkers or for a game of Authors.

∞

It was only a short time until school would start up again. Lynwood was working on his bike in the garage, hoping to have his new bike ready to ride to school on the very first day.

He had painted the bike. "That's a great paint job!" Sarah Beth said, admiring the bright blue bike with a neat silver streak.

"Thanks," said Lynwood. "Tomorrow Dad's going to take me to the bicycle shop to buy new tires. I'll use your gift certificate for something, too. Would you like to go with us?"

Sarah Beth could hardly believe her ears. "Would I ever!" she beamed.

Lynwood had almost finished cleaning and polishing the spokes in the wheels. They already gleamed like new. The original seat cover was made of fine leather. After Lynwood cleaned it and applied some leather cream that Uncle Ben had given him, it, too, looked new.

"I think I have enough money to buy new grips for the handlebars and a new chain, as well as the tires," Lynwood told his sister. "Maybe new pedals, too, although these are still usable."

"What will you get with the gift certificate I gave you?" Sarah Beth asked.

"I don't know yet. That'll depend on how much money is left after I buy the things I really need," he said.

At the bicycle shop, Sarah Beth watched as Lynwood and Daddy chose a good set of tires, some handlebar grips, and a chain. Lynwood added the costs in his head. His smile told his sister that he had more than enough money to pay for these items.

Sarah Beth noticed the delight in her brother's eyes as he examined the horns, the lights, the baskets, and all the gadgets that could be added to the bike. She was kind of hoping he would choose a horn.

At last Lynwood reached a decision. He would add enough of his own money to his sister's gift to buy a basket and a cyclometer to measure the distance he rode.

When they got home, Lynwood and Daddy put the new accessories on the bike. Everybody stood back and admired it. "It looks just as fine as any new bike in the store," Lynwood declared.

Sarah Beth had to agree. Who would have imagined that the crummy piece of junk Daddy had brought home several weeks ago could be transformed into this? She knew the answer to that question, of course. Lynwood had pictured in his mind what a great bike the junk could become.

⚭

The time for Mama's state convention was almost here. The family was gathered in the living room. Sarah Beth was reading a picture book to Will, Daddy was reading the newspaper, Lynwood was painting a picture, and Grandma was darning socks.

Mama came into the room wearing her new dress made from the material Sarah Beth had given her. Daddy laid down the paper and gave a low whistle as Lynwood glanced at Sarah Beth and winked. Sarah Beth grinned.

"You'll be the most beautiful woman at the state convention," Daddy declared.

Mama's eyes twinkled. "At least, I'll be wearing the most beautiful dress," she said.

The dress was almost finished. Mama had added a collar of creamy silk that matched the color of the swirls in the brown fabric. All that remained to be done was the hem. Mama had asked Grandma to hem the dress. All the women in the sewing circle at church said that Grandma sewed the finest hems in the county — maybe the finest in the whole country.

Grandma hadn't said a word since Mama came into the room — and her face gave not the slightest clue to her thoughts. But she laid down the sock she was darning and pinned the hem in place. Tomorrow she would sew it.

⚭

Grandma and Sarah Beth were shelling October beans. The fat, dry beans with the purplish-red stripes would taste good next winter.

"You know, Grandma," Sarah Beth said, "I miss my chickens. I keep thinking every morning and every evening that I should go and feed them."

"You really took good care of those chickens," Grandma commented. "No wonder you miss them. But now you have the money you wanted."

"Yes," Sarah Beth agreed. "And I already have the things I wanted to buy with the money. I guess I shouldn't have counted the things I wanted to buy before the chickens even hatched." She and Grandma both laughed.

"So, what are you going to buy?" Grandma asked.

"I don't know," Sarah Beth replied slowly. Then she said, "Nothing I can buy for myself will bring me more happiness than the things I've already bought and the money I will give to help the boys and girls in Nigeria."

"You have discovered for yourself the truth of an old proverb," Grandma said, laying her hand gently on her granddaughter's shoulder. "'One who gives cheerfully gives twice—once to others, once to oneself.'"

They worked quietly for a little while. Sarah Beth broke the silence. "Why do you think the milkmaid in the fable tripped and spilled the milk?" she asked her grandmother.

"I don't really know," Grandma admitted. "The fable doesn't tell us that."

"No, but I have an idea," Sarah Beth continued. "I think maybe it was because she was thinking only of herself and what she wanted."

Mama interrupted the conversation. She came into the room carrying two of Sarah Beth's school dresses. "Stand up," she said to her daughter, "and let me see how much hem I need to let down in these dresses."

Mama held each of the dresses up to Sarah Beth. "I can hardly believe how much taller you've grown in one short summer," Mama said.

"That's not the only way your daughter has grown this summer," Grandma said with a warm smile.

Sarah Beth returned the smile, too. I do believe, Sarah Beth thought to herself, that Grandma is actually proud of me. No, pleased with me, she corrected herself.

# Nathan's Secret

N. Geraldine Plunkett, author
Beth Gallo, illustrator

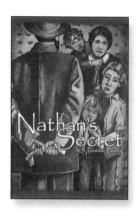

What is a young boy to do when his father must leave home and hide in the woods to escape being forced to fight for the Confederate army? How can Nathan help protect his family? What should he say to friends who think his papa is a coward?

Readers of *Sarah Beth's Problem* will also enjoy *Nathan's Secret*, Gerry Plunkett's first book published by Brethren Press. Also set in rural Virginia, this story reinforces the values of friendship, faith, and peacemaking.

ISBN: 0-87178-029-1
#8291